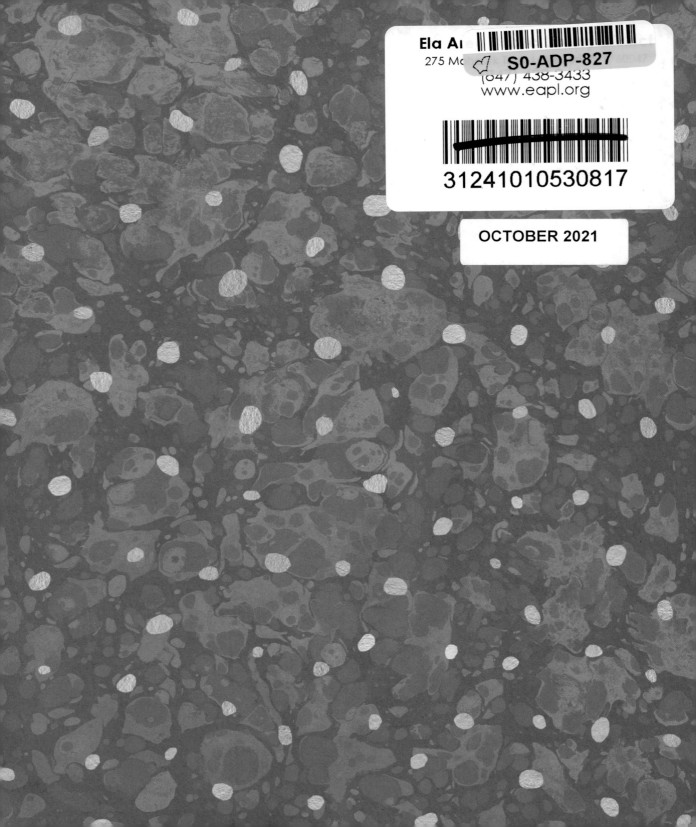

Harry Potter
A Magical Year

THE HARRY POTTER SERIES
In reading order:
Harry Potter and the Sorcerer's Stone
Harry Potter and the Chamber of Secrets
Harry Potter and the Prisoner of Azkaban
Harry Potter and the Goblet of Fire
Harry Potter and the Order of the Phoenix
Harry Potter and the Half-Blood Prince
Harry Potter and the Deathly Hallows

COMPANION VOLUMES
Fantastic Beasts and Where to Find Them
Quidditch Through the Ages
(Published in aid of Comic Relief and Lumos)

The Tales of Beedle the Bard
(Published in aid of Lumos)

The three companion volumes also available as:
The Hogwarts Library
(Published in aid of Comic Relief and Lumos)

ILLUSTRATED EDITIONS
Illustrated by Jim Kay
Harry Potter and the Sorcerer's Stone
Harry Potter and the Chamber of Secrets
Harry Potter and the Prisoner of Azkaban
Harry Potter and the Goblet of Fire

Illustrated by Olivia Lomenech Gill
Fantastic Beasts and Where to Find Them

Illustrated by Lisbeth Zwerger
The Tales of Beedle the Bard

Illustrated by Emily Gravett
Quidditch Through the Ages

Harry Potter
A Magical Year

The Illustrations of
JIM KAY

SCHOLASTIC INC.

Library of Congress Control Number: 2021938438

ISBN 978-1-338-80997-8

10 9 8 7 6 5 4 3 2 1   21 22 23 24 25

Printed in Italy
First edition, October 2021

FSC
www.fsc.org

MIX
Paper from
responsible sources
FSC® C013123

ACKNOWLEDGMENTS

It's strange to think that, back in 2013, a single phone call with an offer of an illustration job would completely change my life and forge friendships in far-flung places, a love for Potter and publishing being the thread that connects us all. I'd like to express my gratitude to the Children's Books team at Bloomsbury, who conceived and put together this book of pieces from the Potter Pile while I've been laboring over *The Order of the Phoenix*. In particular, I'd like to acknowledge the support and patience of Sarah Goodwin, Isabel Ford, Mandy Archer, and Rebecca McNally, who have time and again saved me from difficult and dark places along the way, put up with my changeable temperament with grace, care, and humor, and given me the space to work on this challenging book in my own way.

Particular thanks must also go to Ian Lamb, Alison Eldred, and Val Braithwaite, without whom I wouldn't have a career in "coloring in," which, let's face it, has made me one of the luckiest people alive.

Finally, I am indebted to J.K. Rowling, a living wellspring of creativity who keeps our little boat bobbing along, inspiring and propelling us through her magical world.

Thank you, and lots of love to you all.

*For all of those who have doubts and
depression, you are not alone*
Jim Kay

Contents

January

All in all, they were glad when the rest of the school returned shortly after New Year, and Gryffindor Tower became crowded and noisy again.

JANUARY 1

"Promise me you'll look after yourself.... Stay out of trouble...."

"I always do, Mrs. Weasley," said Harry. "I like a quiet life, you know me."

HARRY POTTER AND THE HALF-BLOOD PRINCE,
Chapter 17, "A Sluggish Memory"

JANUARY 2

Chairs slid backward again as the Knight Bus jumped from the Birmingham motorway to a quiet country lane full of hairpin bends. Hedgerows on either side of the road were leaping out of their way as they mounted the verges. From here they moved to a main street in the middle of a busy town, then to a viaduct surrounded by tall hills, then to a windswept road between high-rise flats, each time with a loud BANG.

"I've changed my mind," muttered Ron, picking himself up from the floor for the sixth time, "I never want to ride on here again."

HARRY POTTER AND THE ORDER OF THE PHOENIX,
Chapter 24, "Occlumency"

JANUARY 3

The six of them struggled up the slippery drive toward the castle dragging their trunks. Hermione was already talking about knitting a few elf hats before bedtime. Harry glanced back when they reached the oak front doors; the Knight Bus had already gone ...

HARRY POTTER AND THE ORDER OF THE PHOENIX,
Chapter 24, "Occlumency"

JANUARY 4

Harry glanced out of the corridor windows
as they passed; the sun was already sinking over
grounds carpeted in deeper snow than had lain
over the Burrow garden. In the distance, he could
see Hagrid feeding Buckbeak in front of his cabin.

HARRY POTTER AND THE HALF-BLOOD PRINCE,
Chapter 17, "A Sluggish Memory"

JANUARY 5

"Oh, hang on — password. *Abstinence*."

"Precisely," said the Fat Lady in a feeble voice,
and swung forward to reveal the portrait hole.

"What's up with her?" asked Harry.

"Overindulged over Christmas, apparently,"
said Hermione, rolling her eyes as she led the
way into the packed common room.

HARRY POTTER AND THE HALF-BLOOD PRINCE,
Chapter 17, "A Sluggish Memory"

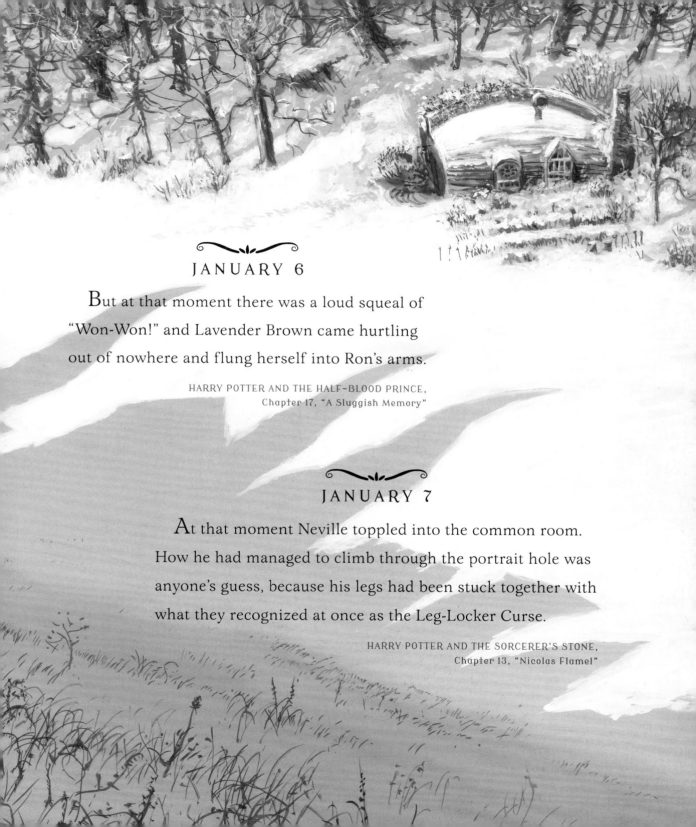

JANUARY 6

But at that moment there was a loud squeal of "Won-Won!" and Lavender Brown came hurtling out of nowhere and flung herself into Ron's arms.

HARRY POTTER AND THE HALF-BLOOD PRINCE,
Chapter 17, "A Sluggish Memory"

JANUARY 7

At that moment Neville toppled into the common room. How he had managed to climb through the portrait hole was anyone's guess, because his legs had been stuck together with what they recognized at once as the Leg-Locker Curse.

HARRY POTTER AND THE SORCERER'S STONE,
Chapter 13, "Nicolas Flamel"

JANUARY 8

"You take *Remedial Potions*?" asked Zacharias Smith superciliously, having cornered Harry in the entrance hall after lunch. "Good Lord, you must be terrible, Snape doesn't usually give extra lessons, does he?"

HARRY POTTER AND THE ORDER OF THE PHOENIX,
Chapter 24, "Occlumency"

JANUARY 9

PROFESSOR SNAPE'S BIRTHDAY

"As there is little foolish wand-waving here, many of you will hardly believe this is magic. I don't expect you will really understand the beauty of the softly simmering cauldron with its shimmering fumes, the delicate power of liquids that creep through human veins, bewitching the mind, ensnaring the senses . . . I can teach you how to bottle fame, brew glory, even stopper death — if you aren't as big a bunch of dunderheads as I usually have to teach."

Severus Snape

HARRY POTTER AND THE SORCERER'S STONE,
Chapter 8, "The Potions Master"

JANUARY 10

"Detention, Saturday night, my office," said Snape.
"I do not take cheek from anyone, Potter . . . not even
'*the Chosen One.*'"

HARRY POTTER AND THE HALF-BLOOD PRINCE,
Chapter 9, "The Half-Blood Prince"

JANUARY 11

Professor Sprout had the *Prophet* propped against a bottle of ketchup and was reading the front page with such concentration that she was not noticing the gentle drip of egg yolk falling into her lap from her stationary spoon.

HARRY POTTER AND THE ORDER OF THE PHOENIX,
Chapter 25, "The Beetle at Bay"

JANUARY 12

It was Professor Trelawney, gliding toward them as though on wheels. She had put on a green sequined dress in honor of the occasion, making her look more than ever like a glittering, oversized dragonfly.

HARRY POTTER AND THE PRISONER OF AZKABAN,
Chapter 11, "The Firebolt"

JANUARY 13

The last thing anyone felt like doing was spending two hours on the grounds on a raw January morning, but Hagrid had provided a bonfire full of salamanders for their enjoyment, and they spent an unusually good lesson collecting dry wood and leaves to keep the fire blazing while the flame-loving lizards scampered up and down the crumbling, white-hot logs.

HARRY POTTER AND THE PRISONER OF AZKABAN,
Chapter 12, "The Patronus"

JANUARY 14

"Well, write it in your homework planner then!" said Hermione encouragingly. "So you don't forget!"

Harry and Ron exchanged looks as he reached into his bag, withdrew the planner and opened it tentatively.

"Don't leave it till later, you big second-rater!" chided the book . . .

HARRY POTTER AND THE ORDER OF THE PHOENIX,
Chapter 24, "Occlumency"

JANUARY 15

Hermione, who was sweaty-faced and had soot on her nose, looked livid. Her half-finished antidote, comprising fifty-two ingredients, including a chunk of her own hair, bubbled sluggishly behind Slughorn, who had eyes for nobody but Harry.

HARRY POTTER AND THE HALF-BLOOD PRINCE,
Chapter 18, "Birthday Surprises"

JANUARY 16

Harry knew that Hermione had meant well, but that didn't stop him from being angry with her. He had been the owner of the best broom in the world for a few short hours, and now, because of her interference, he didn't know whether he would ever see it again.

HARRY POTTER AND THE PRISONER OF AZKABAN,
Chapter 12, "The Patronus"

JANUARY 17

"Ah, Harry, how often this happens, even between the best of friends! Each of us believes that what he has to say is much more important than anything the other might have to contribute!"

Albus Dumbledore

HARRY POTTER AND THE HALF-BLOOD PRINCE,
Chapter 17, "A Sluggish Memory"

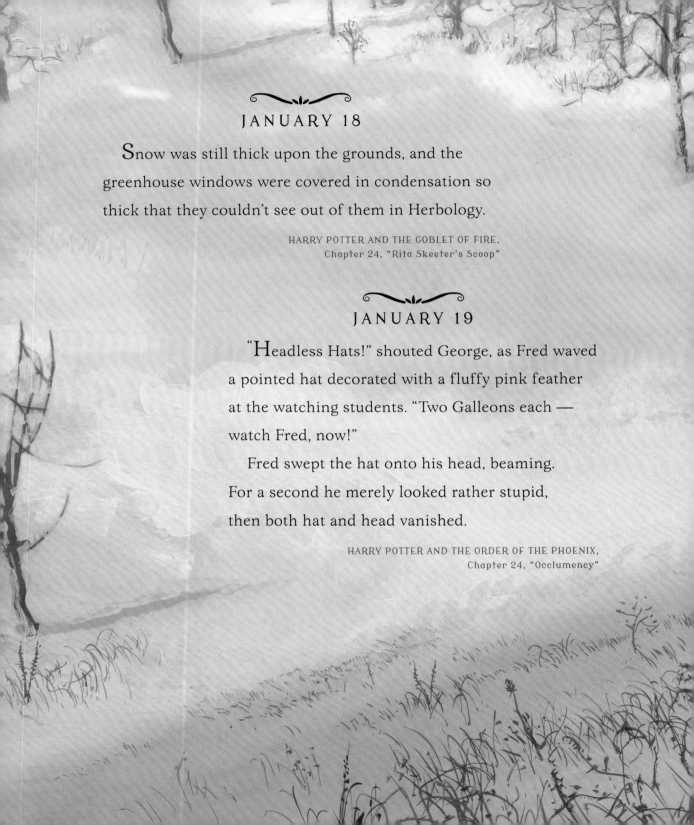

JANUARY 18

Snow was still thick upon the grounds, and the greenhouse windows were covered in condensation so thick that they couldn't see out of them in Herbology.

HARRY POTTER AND THE GOBLET OF FIRE,
Chapter 24, "Rita Skeeter's Scoop"

JANUARY 19

"Headless Hats!" shouted George, as Fred waved a pointed hat decorated with a fluffy pink feather at the watching students. "Two Galleons each — watch Fred, now!"

Fred swept the hat onto his head, beaming. For a second he merely looked rather stupid, then both hat and head vanished.

HARRY POTTER AND THE ORDER OF THE PHOENIX,
Chapter 24, "Occlumency"

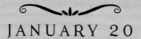

JANUARY 20

"What does a Patronus look like?" said Harry curiously.

"Each one is unique to the wizard who conjures it."

HARRY POTTER AND THE PRISONER OF AZKABAN,
Chapter 12, "The Patronus"

JANUARY 21

So many students filed past the hospital wing trying to catch a glimpse of her that Madam Pomfrey took out her curtains again and placed them around Hermione's bed, to spare her the shame of being seen with a furry face.

Harry and Ron went to visit her every evening. When the new term started, they brought her each day's homework.

"If I'd sprouted whiskers, I'd take a break from work," said Ron, tipping a stack of books onto Hermione's bedside table one evening.

HARRY POTTER AND THE CHAMBER OF SECRETS,
Chapter 13, "The Very Secret Diary"

JANUARY 22

As they passed the Durmstrang ship moored in the lake, they saw Viktor Krum emerge onto the deck, dressed in nothing but swimming trunks. He was very skinny indeed, but apparently a lot tougher than he looked, because he climbed up onto the side of the ship, stretched out his arms, and dived, right into the lake.

HARRY POTTER AND THE GOBLET OF FIRE,
Chapter 24, "Rita Skeeter's Scoop"

JANUARY 23

Harry took a great breath and slid under the surface — and now, sitting on the marble bottom of the bubble-filled bath, he heard a chorus of eerie voices singing to him from the open egg in his hands . . .

HARRY POTTER AND THE GOBLET OF FIRE,
Chapter 25, "The Egg and the Eye"

JANUARY 24

Myrtle puffed herself up and shrieked, "Let's all throw books at Myrtle, because *she* can't feel it! Ten points if you can get it through her stomach! Fifty points if it goes through her head! Well, ha, ha, ha! What a lovely game, I *don't* think!"

HARRY POTTER AND THE CHAMBER OF SECRETS,
Chapter 13, "The Very Secret Diary"

JANUARY 25

Wood was working the team harder than
ever. Even the endless rain that had replaced
the snow couldn't dampen his spirits. The Weasleys
complained that Wood was becoming a fanatic, but Harry
was on Wood's side. If they won their next match, against
Hufflepuff, they would overtake Slytherin in the House
Championship for the first time in seven years.

HARRY POTTER AND THE SORCERER'S STONE,
Chapter 13, "Nicolas Flamel"

JANUARY 26

PROFESSOR LOCKHART'S BIRTHDAY

"Come on now — round them up, round
them up, they're only pixies," Lockhart shouted.
He rolled up his sleeves, brandished his
wand, and bellowed, *"Peskipiksi Pesternomi!"*
It had absolutely no effect; one of the
pixies seized his wand and threw
it out of the window, too.

HARRY POTTER AND THE CHAMBER OF SECRETS,
Chapter 6, "Gilderoy Lockhart"

JANUARY 27

"You'd be surprised," said Ron, who was looking apprehensively at the book. "Some of the books the Ministry's confiscated — Dad's told me — there was one that burned your eyes out. And everyone who read *Sonnets of a Sorcerer* spoke in limericks for the rest of their lives. And some old witch in Bath had a book that you could *never stop reading*!"

HARRY POTTER AND THE CHAMBER OF SECRETS,
Chapter 13, "The Very Secret Diary"

JANUARY 28

"The truth." Dumbledore sighed. "It is a beautiful and terrible thing, and should therefore be treated with great caution. However, I shall answer your questions unless I have a very good reason not to, in which case I beg you'll forgive me. I shall not, of course, lie."

HARRY POTTER AND THE SORCERER'S STONE,
Chapter 17, "The Man with Two Faces"

JANUARY 29

"You think the dead we have loved ever truly leave us? You think that we don't recall them more clearly than ever in times of great trouble?"

Albus Dumbledore

HARRY POTTER AND THE PRISONER OF AZKABAN,
Chapter 22, "Owl Post Again"

JANUARY 30

LILY POTTER'S BIRTHDAY

"Your mother died to save you. If there is one thing Voldemort cannot understand, it is love. He didn't realize that love as powerful as your mother's for you leaves its own mark. Not a scar, no visible sign . . . to have been loved so deeply, even though the person who loved us is gone, will give us some protection forever. It is in your very skin."

Albus Dumbledore

HARRY POTTER AND THE SORCERER'S STONE,
Chapter 17, "The Man with Two Faces"

JANUARY 31

The lamps in Dumbledore's office were lit, the portraits of previous headmasters were snoring gently in their frames, and the Pensieve was ready upon the desk once more.

HARRY POTTER AND THE HALF-BLOOD PRINCE,
Chapter 17, "A Sluggish Memory"

February

The snow melted around the school
as February arrived, to be replaced
by cold, dreary wetness.

FEBRUARY 1

"Oh it's so beautiful!" whispered Lavender Brown. "How did she get it? They're supposed to be really hard to catch!"

The unicorn was so brightly white it made the snow all around look gray. It was pawing the ground nervously with its golden hooves and throwing back its horned head.

HARRY POTTER AND THE GOBLET OF FIRE,
Chapter 24, "Rita Skeeter's Scoop"

FEBRUARY 2

"Here you go," said Harry, handing Ron the Firebolt.

Ron, an expression of ecstasy on his face, mounted the broom and zoomed off into the gathering darkness while Harry walked around the edge of the field, watching him.

HARRY POTTER AND THE PRISONER OF AZKABAN,
Chapter 13, "Gryffindor Versus Ravenclaw"

FEBRUARY 3

"You all know, of course, that Hogwarts was founded over a thousand years ago — the precise date is uncertain — by the four greatest witches and wizards of the age."

Professor Binns

HARRY POTTER AND THE CHAMBER OF SECRETS,
Chapter 9, "The Writing on the Wall"

FEBRUARY 4

He sprinted back to the one-eyed witch, opened her hump, heaved himself inside, and slid down to meet his bag at the bottom of the stone chute. He wiped the Marauder's Map blank again, then set off at a run.

HARRY POTTER AND THE PRISONER OF AZKABAN,
Chapter 14, "Snape's Grudge"

FEBRUARY 5

"They run off eckeltricity, do they?" he said knowledgeably. "Ah yes, I can see the plugs. I collect plugs," he added to Uncle Vernon. "And batteries. Got a very large collection of batteries. My wife thinks I'm mad, but there you are."

HARRY POTTER AND THE GOBLET OF FIRE,
Chapter 4, "Back to the Burrow"

FEBRUARY 6

ARTHUR WEASLEY'S BIRTHDAY

"*Your sons flew that car to Harry's house and back last night!*" shouted Mrs. Weasley. "What have you got to say about that, eh?"

"Did you really?" said Mr. Weasley eagerly. "Did it go all right? I — I mean," he faltered, as sparks flew from Mrs. Weasley's eyes, "that — that was very wrong, boys — very wrong indeed...."

HARRY POTTER AND THE CHAMBER OF SECRETS,
Chapter 3, "The Burrow"

FEBRUARY 7

"Never trust anything that can think for itself

if you can't see where it keeps its brain."

Arthur Weasley

HARRY POTTER AND THE CHAMBER OF SECRETS,
Chapter 18, "Dobby's Reward"

FEBRUARY 8

"'Third regurgitating public toilet reported in Bethnal Green, kindly investigate immediately.' This is getting ridiculous. . . ."

"A regurgitating toilet?"

"Anti-Muggle pranksters," said Mr. Weasley, frowning. "We had two last week, one in Wimbledon, one in Elephant and Castle. Muggles are pulling the flush and instead of everything disappearing — well, you can imagine."

HARRY POTTER AND THE ORDER OF THE PHOENIX,
Chapter 7, "The Ministry of Magic"

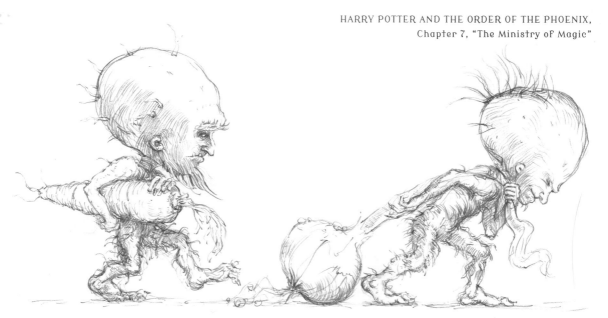

FEBRUARY 9

"They're working to bring down the Ministry of Magic from within using a combination of Dark Magic and gum disease."

Luna Lovegood

HARRY POTTER AND THE HALF-BLOOD PRINCE,
Chapter 15, "The Unbreakable Vow"

FEBRUARY 10

"Wrackspurt got you?" asked Luna sympathetically, peering at Harry through her enormous colored spectacles.

HARRY POTTER AND THE HALF-BLOOD PRINCE,
Chapter 7, "The Slug Club"

FEBRUARY 11

"How come people hide your stuff?" he asked her, frowning.

"Oh . . . well . . ." She shrugged. "I think they think I'm a bit odd, you know. Some people call me 'Loony' Lovegood, actually."

HARRY POTTER AND THE ORDER OF THE PHOENIX,
Chapter 38, "The Second War Begins"

FEBRUARY 12

"Daddy, look — one of the gnomes actually bit me!"

"How wonderful! Gnome saliva is enormously beneficial!" said Mr. Lovegood, seizing Luna's outstretched finger and examining the bleeding puncture marks. "Luna, my love, if you should feel any burgeoning talent today — perhaps an unexpected urge to sing opera or to declaim in Mermish — do not repress it! You may have been gifted by the Gernumblies!"

HARRY POTTER AND THE DEATHLY HALLOWS,
Chapter 8, "The Wedding"

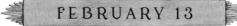
FEBRUARY 13

LUNA LOVEGOOD'S BIRTHDAY

"You're not going mad or anything. I can see them too."

"Can you?" said Harry desperately, turning to Luna. He could see the bat-winged horses reflected in her wide, silvery eyes.

"Oh yes," said Luna, "I've been able to see them ever since my first day here. They've always pulled the carriages. Don't worry. You're just as sane as I am."

HARRY POTTER AND THE ORDER OF THE PHOENIX,
Chapter 10, "Luna Lovegood"

FEBRUARY 14

VALENTINE'S DAY

Losing his head, Harry tried to make a run for it, but the dwarf seized him around the knees and brought him crashing to the floor.

"Right," he said, sitting on Harry's ankles, "here is your singing valentine:

"*His eyes are as green as a fresh pickled toad,*

His hair is as dark as a blackboard.

I wish he was mine, he's really divine,

The hero who conquered the Dark Lord."

HARRY POTTER AND THE CHAMBER OF SECRETS,
Chapter 13, "The Very Secret Diary"

38

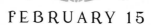

FEBRUARY 15

"You should write a book," Ron told Hermione as he cut up his potatoes, "translating mad things girls do so boys can understand them."

HARRY POTTER AND THE ORDER OF THE PHOENIX,
Chapter 26, "Seen and Unforeseen"

FEBRUARY 16

"Sir Cadogan, did you just let a man enter Gryffindor Tower?"

"Certainly, good lady!" cried Sir Cadogan.

There was a stunned silence, both inside and outside the common room.

"You — you *did*?" said Professor McGonagall. "But — but the password!"

"He had 'em!" said Sir Cadogan proudly. "Had the whole week's, my lady! Read 'em off a little piece of paper!"

HARRY POTTER AND THE PRISONER OF AZKABAN,
Chapter 13, "Gryffindor Versus Ravenclaw"

FEBRUARY 17

"Oooh, it might have hidden powers," said Hermione enthusiastically, taking the diary and looking at it closely.

"If it has, it's hiding them very well," said Ron. "Maybe it's shy. I don't know why you don't chuck it, Harry."

HARRY POTTER AND THE CHAMBER OF SECRETS,
Chapter 13, "The Very Secret Diary"

FEBRUARY 18

The pages of the diary began to blow as though caught in a high wind, stopping halfway through the month of June. Mouth hanging open, Harry saw that the little square for June thirteenth seemed to have turned into a minuscule television screen. His hands trembling slightly, he raised the book to press his eye against the little window, and before he knew what was happening, he was tilting forward; the window was widening, he felt his body leave his bed, and he was pitched headfirst through the opening in the page, into a whirl of color and shadow.

HARRY POTTER AND THE CHAMBER OF SECRETS,
Chapter 13, "The Very Secret Diary"

FEBRUARY 19

"Ah, well, people can be a bit stupid abou' their pets," said Hagrid wisely.

HARRY POTTER AND THE PRISONER OF AZKABAN,
Chapter 14, "Snape's Grudge"

FEBRUARY 20

The first thing they saw on entering Hagrid's cabin was Buckbeak, who was stretched out on top of Hagrid's patchwork quilt, his enormous wings folded tight to his body, enjoying a large plate of dead ferrets. Averting his eyes from this unpleasant sight, Harry saw a gigantic, hairy brown suit and a very horrible yellow-and-orange tie hanging from the top of Hagrid's wardrobe door.

HARRY POTTER AND THE PRISONER OF AZKABAN,
Chapter 14, "Snape's Grudge"

FEBRUARY 21

Hagrid poured them tea and offered them a plate of Bath buns, but they knew better than to accept; they had had too much experience with Hagrid's cooking.

HARRY POTTER AND THE PRISONER OF AZKABAN,
Chapter 14, "Snape's Grudge"

FEBRUARY 22

The lake, which Harry had always taken for granted as just another feature of the grounds, drew his eyes whenever he was near a classroom window, a great, iron-gray mass of chilly water, whose dark and icy depths were starting to seem as distant as the moon.

HARRY POTTER AND THE GOBLET OF FIRE,
Chapter 26, "The Second Task"

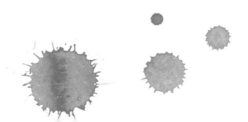

FEBRUARY 23

Harry returned to the Gryffindor common room, pulled a table into a corner, and continued to search. There was nothing in *Madcap Magic for Wacky Warlocks* . . . nothing in *A Guide to Medieval Sorcery* . . . not one mention of underwater exploits in *An Anthology of Eighteenth-Century Charms*, or in *Dreadful Denizens of the Deep*, or *Powers You Never Knew You Had and What to Do With Them Now You've Wised Up*.

HARRY POTTER AND THE GOBLET OF FIRE,
Chapter 26, "The Second Task"

FEBRUARY 24
TRIWIZARD TOURNAMENT
THE SECOND TASK

"You has to eat this, sir!" squeaked the elf, and he put his hand in the pocket of his shorts and drew out a ball of what looked like slimy, grayish-green rat tails. "Right before you go into the lake, sir — gillyweed!"

"What's it do?" said Harry, staring at the gillyweed.

"It will make Harry Potter breathe underwater, sir!"

HARRY POTTER AND THE GOBLET OF FIRE,
Chapter 26, "The Second Task"

FEBRUARY 25

They walked in silence to the door of Moody's office, where he stopped and looked up at Harry.

"You ever thought of a career as an Auror, Potter?"

HARRY POTTER AND THE GOBLET OF FIRE,
Chapter 25, "The Egg and the Eye"

FEBRUARY 26

"Thank you," said Twycross. "Now then . . ."

He waved his wand. Old-fashioned wooden hoops instantly appeared on the floor in front of every student.

"The important things to remember when Apparating are the three D's!" said Twycross. "Destination, Determination, Deliberation!"

HARRY POTTER AND THE HALF-BLOOD PRINCE,
Chapter 18, "Birthday Surprises"

FEBRUARY 27

The school owls swooped into the Great Hall, carrying the mail as usual, and Neville choked as a huge barn owl landed in front of him, a scarlet envelope clutched in its beak. Harry and Ron, who were sitting opposite him, recognized the letter as a Howler at once — Ron had got one from his mother the year before.

"Run for it, Neville," Ron advised.

HARRY POTTER AND THE PRISONER OF AZKABAN,
Chapter 14, "Snape's Grudge"

FEBRUARY 28

A little way to his left, Ernie Macmillan was contemplating his hoop so hard that his face had turned pink; it looked as though he was straining to lay a Quaffle-sized egg.

HARRY POTTER AND THE HALF-BLOOD PRINCE,
Chapter 18, "Birthday Surprises"

FEBRUARY 29

"I am sorry to say that from the moment you have arrived in this class, my *dear*, it has been apparent that you do not have what the noble art of Divination requires. Indeed, I don't remember ever meeting a student whose mind was so hopelessly mundane."

There was a moment's silence. Then —

"Fine!" said Hermione suddenly, getting up and cramming *Unfogging the Future* back into her bag. "Fine!" she repeated, swinging the bag over her shoulder and almost knocking Ron off his chair. "I give up! I'm leaving!"

HARRY POTTER AND THE PRISONER OF AZKABAN,
Chapter 15, "The Quidditch Final"

HERBOLOGY
EXAMS
This Way ➡

March

In March several of the Mandrakes threw a
loud and raucous party in greenhouse three.
This made Professor Sprout very happy.

MARCH 1

"You never get anything new, either, with five brothers. I've got Bill's old robes, Charlie's old wand, and Percy's old rat."

Ron Weasley

HARRY POTTER AND THE SORCERER'S STONE,
Chapter 6, "The Journey from Platform Nine and Three-Quarters"

MARCH 2

"Your Wheezy, sir, your Wheezy — Wheezy who is giving Dobby his sweater!"

Dobby plucked at the shrunken maroon sweater he was now wearing over his shorts.

"*What?*" Harry gasped. "They've got . . . they've got *Ron*?"

"The thing Harry Potter will miss most, sir!" squeaked Dobby.

HARRY POTTER AND THE GOBLET OF FIRE,
Chapter 26, "The Second Task"

MARCH 3

"One person can't feel all that at once, they'd explode."

Ron Weasley

HARRY POTTER AND THE ORDER OF THE PHOENIX,
Chapter 21, "The Eye of the Snake"

MARCH 4

"It sort of floated toward me," said Ron, illustrating the movement with his free index finger, "right to my chest, and then — it just went straight through. It was here," he touched a point close to his heart, "I could feel it, it was hot. And once it was inside me I knew what I was supposed to do, I knew it would take me where I needed to go."

HARRY POTTER AND THE DEATHLY HALLOWS,
Chapter 19, "The Silver Doe"

MARCH 5

Everything was lit with a dim, crimson light; the curtains at the windows were all closed, and the many lamps were draped with dark red scarves. It was stiflingly warm, and the fire which was burning under the crowded mantelpiece was giving off a heavy, sickly sort of perfume as it heated a large copper kettle.

HARRY POTTER AND THE PRISONER OF AZKABAN,
Chapter 6, "Talons and Tea Leaves"

MARCH 6

"How nice to see you in the physical world at last."

Sybill Trelawney

HARRY POTTER AND THE PRISONER OF AZKABAN,
Chapter 6, "Talons and Tea Leaves"

MARCH 7

"I have been crystal gazing, Headmaster," said Professor Trelawney, in her mistiest, most faraway voice, "and to my astonishment, I saw myself abandoning my solitary luncheon and coming to join you. Who am I to refuse the promptings of fate?"

HARRY POTTER AND THE PRISONER OF AZKABAN,
Chapter 11, "The Firebolt"

MARCH 8

"You know," said Ron, whose hair was on end because of all the times he had run his fingers through it in frustration, "I think it's back to the old Divination standby."

"What — make it up?"

HARRY POTTER AND THE GOBLET OF FIRE,
Chapter 14, "The Unforgivable Curses"

MARCH 9

PROFESSOR TRELAWNEY'S BIRTHDAY

"You — you just told me that the — the Dark Lord's going to rise again . . . that his servant's going to go back to him. . . ."

Professor Trelawney looked thoroughly startled.

"The Dark Lord? He-Who-Must-Not-Be-Named? My dear boy, that's hardly something to joke about. . . . Rise again, indeed —"

HARRY POTTER AND THE PRISONER OF AZKABAN,
Chapter 16, "Professor Trelawney's Prediction"

MARCH 10

There was a loud crack, and Harry's cloudy Patronus vanished along with the dementor; he sank into a chair, feeling as exhausted as if he'd just run a mile, and felt his legs shaking. Out of the corner of his eye, he saw Professor Lupin forcing the boggart back into the packing case with his wand; it had turned into a silvery orb again.

HARRY POTTER AND THE PRISONER OF AZKABAN,
Chapter 12, "The Patronus"

MARCH 11

Professor Lupin had raised his eyebrows.

"I was hoping that Neville would assist me with the first stage of the operation," he said, "and I am sure he will perform it admirably."

HARRY POTTER AND THE PRISONER OF AZKABAN,
Chapter 7, "The Boggart in the Wardrobe"

MARCH 12

"Professor Snape has very kindly concocted a potion for me," he said. "I have never been much of a potion-brewer and this one is particularly complex." He picked up the goblet and sniffed it. "Pity sugar makes it useless," he added, taking a sip and shuddering.

HARRY POTTER AND THE PRISONER OF AZKABAN,
Chapter 8, "Flight of the Fat Lady"

MARCH 13

There were delays in the post because the owls kept being blown off course. The brown owl that Harry had sent to Sirius with the dates of the Hogsmeade weekend turned up at breakfast on Friday morning with half its feathers sticking up the wrong way . . .

HARRY POTTER AND THE GOBLET OF FIRE,
Chapter 27, "Padfoot Returns"

MARCH 14

The snowy owl clicked her beak and fluttered down onto Harry's arm.

"Very smart owl you've got there," chuckled Tom. "Arrived about five minutes after you did."

HARRY POTTER AND THE PRISONER OF AZKABAN,
Chapter 3, "The Knight Bus"

MARCH 15

Pigwidgeon was much too small to carry an entire ham up to the mountain by himself, so Harry enlisted the help of two school screech owls as well.

HARRY POTTER AND THE GOBLET OF FIRE,
Chapter 28, "The Madness of Mr. Crouch"

MARCH 16

Frowning, he made to take the letter from the owl, but before he could do so, three, four, five more owls had fluttered down beside it and were jockeying for position, treading in the butter, knocking over the salt, and each attempting to give him their letters first.

"What's going on?" Ron asked in amazement, as the whole of Gryffindor table leaned forward to watch as another seven owls landed amongst the first ones, screeching, hooting, and flapping their wings.

HARRY POTTER AND THE ORDER OF THE PHOENIX,
Chapter 26, "Seen and Unforeseen"

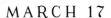

MARCH 17

It was Peeves the Poltergeist, bobbing over the crowd and looking delighted, as he always did, at the sight of wreckage or worry.

HARRY POTTER AND THE PRISONER OF AZKABAN,
Chapter 8, "Flight of the Fat Lady"

MARCH 18

"Not doing nothing!" cackled Peeves, lobbing a water bomb at several fifth-year girls, who screamed and dived into the Great Hall. "Already wet, aren't they? Little squirts! Wheeeeeeeeee!" And he aimed another bomb at a group of second years who had just arrived.

HARRY POTTER AND THE GOBLET OF FIRE,
Chapter 12, "The Triwizard Tournament"

MARCH 19

Harry aimed his wand at Peeves and said, *"Langlock!"* Peeves clutched at his throat, gulped, then swooped from the room making obscene gestures but unable to speak, owing to the fact that his tongue had just glued itself to the roof of his mouth.

"Nice one," said Ron appreciatively . . .

HARRY POTTER AND THE HALF-BLOOD PRINCE,
Chapter 19, "Elf Tails"

MARCH 20

As the teachers bent over Justin and Nearly Headless Nick, examining them, Peeves broke into song:

"Oh Potter, you rotter, oh, what have you done?
You're killing off students, you think it's good fun —"

HARRY POTTER AND THE CHAMBER OF SECRETS,
Chapter 11, "The Dueling Club"

MARCH 21

"Hermione, is there any point in telling you to drop this?" said Ron.

"No!" said Hermione stubbornly. "I want to know how she heard me talking to Viktor! *And* how she found out about Hagrid's mum!"

"Maybe she had you bugged," said Harry.

"Bugged?" said Ron blankly. "What . . . put fleas on her or something?"

HARRY POTTER AND THE GOBLET OF FIRE,
Chapter 28, "The Madness of Mr. Crouch"

MARCH 22

Rita did not say anything for a while, but eyed Hermione shrewdly, her head a little to one side.

"All right, let's say for a moment I'll do it," she said abruptly. "What kind of fee am I going to get?"

"I don't think Daddy exactly pays people to write for the magazine," said Luna dreamily. "They do it because it's an honor and, of course, to see their names in print."

HARRY POTTER AND THE ORDER OF THE PHOENIX,
Chapter 25, "The Beetle at Bay"

MARCH 23

"Let us begin," said Firenze. He swished his long palomino tail, raised his hand toward the leafy canopy overhead then lowered it slowly, and as he did so, the light in the room dimmed, so that they now seemed to be sitting in a forest clearing by twilight, and stars emerged upon the ceiling.

There were *oohs* and gasps, and Ron said audibly, "Blimey!"

"Lie back upon the floor," said Firenze in his calm voice, "and observe the heavens. Here is written, for those who can see, the fortune of our races."

HARRY POTTER AND THE ORDER OF THE PHOENIX,
Chapter 27, "The Centaur and the Sneak"

MARCH 24

The winding lane was leading them out into the wild countryside around Hogsmeade. The cottages were fewer here, and their gardens larger; they were walking toward the foot of the mountain in whose shadow Hogsmeade lay. Then they turned a corner and saw a stile at the end of the lane. Waiting for them, its front paws on the topmost bar, was a very large, shaggy black dog, which was carrying some newspapers in its mouth and looking very familiar. . . .

"Hello, Sirius," said Harry when they had reached him.

HARRY POTTER AND THE GOBLET OF FIRE,
Chapter 27, "Padfoot Returns"

MARCH 25

"Poor old Snuffles," said Ron, breathing deeply. "He must really like you, Harry . . . Imagine having to live off rats."

HARRY POTTER AND THE GOBLET OF FIRE,
Chapter 27, "Padfoot Returns"

MARCH 26

"'The Boy Who Lived' remains a symbol of everything for which we are fighting: the triumph of good, the power of innocence, the need to keep resisting."

Remus Lupin

HARRY POTTER AND THE DEATHLY HALLOWS,
Chapter 22, "The Deathly Hallows"

MARCH 27

"Your father is alive in you, Harry, and shows himself most plainly when you have need of him."
Albus Dumbledore

HARRY POTTER AND THE PRISONER OF AZKABAN,
Chapter 22, *"Owl Post Again"*

MARCH 28

"I'm sorry," he whispered, "I didn't mean to offend you or anything —"

"Offend Dobby!" choked the elf. "Dobby has *never* been asked to sit down by a wizard — like an *equal* —"

HARRY POTTER AND THE CHAMBER OF SECRETS,
Chapter 2, "Dobby's Warning"

MARCH 29

They went into Gladrags Wizardwear to buy a present for Dobby, where they had fun selecting all the most lurid socks they could find, including a pair patterned with flashing gold and silver stars, and another that screamed loudly when they became too smelly.

HARRY POTTER AND THE GOBLET OF FIRE,
Chapter 27, "Padfoot Returns"

MARCH 30

"Kreacher will not insult Harry Potter in front of Dobby, no he won't, or Dobby will shut Kreacher's mouth for him!" cried Dobby in a high-pitched voice.

HARRY POTTER AND THE HALF-BLOOD PRINCE,
Chapter 19, "Elf Tails"

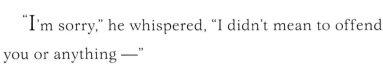

MARCH 31

"Dobby has no master!" squealed the elf. "Dobby is a free elf, and Dobby has come to save Harry Potter and his friends!"

HARRY POTTER AND THE DEATHLY HALLOWS,
Chapter 23, "Malfoy Manor"

April

The weather grew breezier, brighter, and warmer as the holidays passed, but Harry was stuck with the rest of the fifth and seventh years, who were all trapped inside, traipsing back and forth to the library.

"The thing about growing up with Fred and George,"
said Ginny thoughtfully, "is that you sort of start thinking
anything's possible if you've got enough nerve."

HARRY POTTER AND THE ORDER OF THE PHOENIX,
Chapter 29, "Career Advice"

APRIL 2

"E for 'Exceeds Expectations.'
And I've always thought Fred
and I should've got E in
everything, because we
exceeded expectations just
by turning up for the exams."

George Weasley

HARRY POTTER AND THE ORDER
OF THE PHOENIX,
Chapter 15, "The Hogwarts High Inquisitor"

APRIL 3

"Give her hell from us, Peeves."

And Peeves, whom Harry had never seen take an order from a student before, swept his belled hat from his head and sprang to a salute as Fred and George wheeled about to tumultuous applause from the students below and sped out of the open front doors into the glorious sunset.

HARRY POTTER AND THE ORDER OF THE PHOENIX,
Chapter 29, "Career Advice"

APRIL 4

"I believe your friends Misters Fred and George Weasley were responsible for trying to send you a toilet seat. No doubt they thought it would amuse you. Madam Pomfrey, however, felt it might not be very hygienic, and confiscated it."

Albus Dumbledore

HARRY POTTER AND THE SORCERER'S STONE,
Chapter 17, "The Man with Two Faces"

APRIL 5

"Anyone can speak Troll," said Fred dismissively. "All you have to do is point and grunt."

HARRY POTTER AND THE GOBLET OF FIRE,
Chapter 7, "Bagman and Crouch"

APRIL 6

The grounds were still and quiet. No breath of wind disturbed the treetops in the Forbidden Forest; the Whomping Willow was motionless and innocent-looking. It looked as though the conditions for the match would be perfect.

HARRY POTTER AND THE PRISONER OF AZKABAN,
Chapter 15, "The Quidditch Final"

APRIL 7

"Mount your brooms . . . on my whistle . . . three — two — one —"

Madam Hooch

HARRY POTTER AND THE PRISONER OF AZKABAN,
Chapter 13, "Gryffindor Versus Ravenclaw"

APRIL 8

Up in the air, Snape turned on his broomstick just in time to see something scarlet shoot past him, missing him by inches — the next second, Harry had pulled out of the dive, his arm raised in triumph, the Snitch clasped in his hand.

The stands erupted; it had to be a record, no one could ever remember the Snitch being caught so quickly.

HARRY POTTER AND THE SORCERER'S STONE,
Chapter 13, "Nicolas Flamel"

APRIL 9

"And that's Smith of Hufflepuff with the Quaffle," said a dreamy voice, echoing over the grounds. "He did the commentary last time, of course, and Ginny Weasley flew into him, I think probably on purpose, it looked like it. Smith was being quite rude about Gryffindor, I expect he regrets that now he's playing them — oh, look, he's lost the Quaffle, Ginny took it from him, I do like her, she's very nice. . . ."

Luna Lovegood

HARRY POTTER AND THE HALF-BLOOD PRINCE,
Chapter 19, "Elf Tails"

APRIL 10

"It's Easter eggs from Mum," said Ginny.
"There's one for you.... There you go...."
She handed him a handsome chocolate egg
decorated with small, iced Snitches and, according
to the packaging, containing a bag of Fizzing Whizbees.

HARRY POTTER AND THE ORDER OF THE PHOENIX,
Chapter 29, "Career Advice"

APRIL 11

"Oh, why don't we have a night off?" said Hermione brightly, as a
silver-tailed Weasley rocket zoomed past the window. "After all, the
Easter holidays start on Friday, we'll have plenty of time then...."
"Are you feeling all right?" Ron asked, staring at her in disbelief.

HARRY POTTER AND THE ORDER OF THE PHOENIX,
Chapter 28, "Snape's Worst Memory"

APRIL 12

Fred and George Weasley disappeared for a couple of hours
and returned with armfuls of bottles of butterbeer, pumpkin
fizz, and several bags full of Honeydukes sweets.

HARRY POTTER AND THE PRISONER OF AZKABAN,
Chapter 13, "Gryffindor Versus Ravenclaw"

APRIL 13

Madam Pince was swooping down upon them, her shriveled face contorted with rage.

"*Chocolate in the library!*" she screamed. "Out — *out* — OUT!"

And whipping out her wand, she caused Harry's books, bag, and ink bottle to chase him and Ginny from the library, whacking them repeatedly over the head as they ran.

HARRY POTTER AND THE ORDER OF THE PHOENIX,
Chapter 29, "Career Advice"

APRIL 14

It was the first day of the Easter holidays and Hermione, as was her custom, had spent a large part of the day drawing up study schedules for the three of them. Harry and Ron had let her do it — it was easier than arguing with her and, in any case, they might come in useful.

HARRY POTTER AND THE ORDER OF THE PHOENIX,
Chapter 29, "Career Advice"

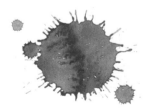

APRIL 15

"*Nearly* Headless? How can you be *nearly* headless?"

Sir Nicholas looked extremely miffed, as if their little chat wasn't going at all the way he wanted.

"Like *this*," he said irritably. He seized his left ear and pulled. His whole head swung off his neck and fell onto his shoulder as if it was on a hinge.

HARRY POTTER AND THE SORCERER'S STONE,
Chapter 7, "The Sorting Hat"

APRIL 16

"Harry! My dear boy!"

Nick made to grasp Harry's hands with both of his own: Harry's felt as though they had been thrust into icy water.

HARRY POTTER AND THE DEATHLY HALLOWS,
Chapter 31, "The Battle of Hogwarts"

APRIL 17

"I know nothing of the secrets of death, Harry, for I chose my feeble imitation of life instead. I believe learned wizards study the matter in the Department of Mysteries —"
Nearly Headless Nick

HARRY POTTER AND THE ORDER OF THE PHOENIX,
Chapter 38, "The Second War Begins"

APRIL 18

Harry took out his wand, murmured, *"Lumos!"* and a tiny light appeared at the end of it, just enough to let them watch the path for signs of spiders.

HARRY POTTER AND THE CHAMBER OF SECRETS,
Chapter 15, "Aragog"

APRIL 19

"I had him from an egg, yeh know," said Hagrid morosely. "Tiny little thing he was when he hatched. 'Bout the size of a Pekingese."

HARRY POTTER AND THE HALF-BLOOD PRINCE,
Chapter 22, "After the Burial"

APRIL 20
DEATH OF ARAGOG

"One for Harry . . ." said Slughorn, dividing a second bottle between two mugs, ". . . and one for me. Well" — he raised his mug high — "to Aragog."

"Aragog," said Harry and Hagrid together.

HARRY POTTER AND THE HALF-BLOOD PRINCE,
Chapter 22, "After the Burial"

APRIL 21

Harry noticed him glance at the fire. Harry looked at it, too.
"Hagrid — what's *that*?"

But he already knew what it was. In the very heart of the fire, underneath the kettle, was a huge, black egg.

HARRY POTTER AND THE SORCERER'S STONE,
Chapter 14, "Norbert the Norwegian Ridgeback"

APRIL 22

All at once there was a scraping noise and the egg split open.
The baby dragon flopped onto the table. It wasn't exactly pretty;
Harry thought it looked like a crumpled, black umbrella.

HARRY POTTER AND THE SORCERER'S STONE,
Chapter 14, "Norbert the Norwegian Ridgeback"

APRIL 23

"Isn't he *beautiful*?" Hagrid murmured. He reached out a hand to stroke
the dragon's head. It snapped at his fingers, showing pointed fangs.

"Bless him, look, he knows his mummy!" said Hagrid.

HARRY POTTER AND THE SORCERER'S STONE,
Chapter 14, "Norbert the Norwegian Ridgeback"

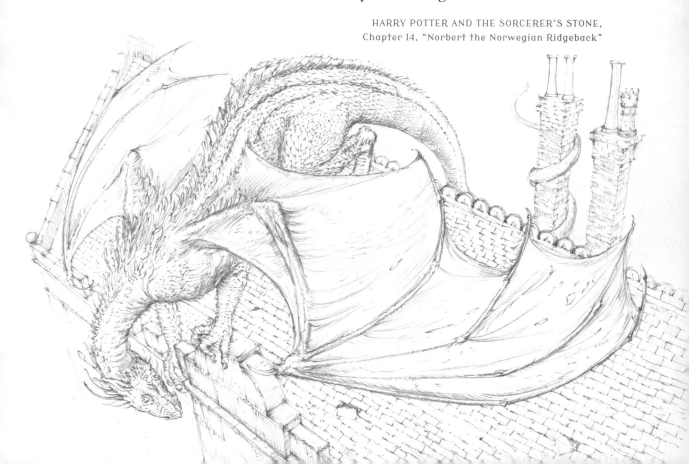

APRIL 24

"Got this outta the library — *Dragon Breeding for Pleasure and Profit* — it's a bit outta date, o' course, but it's all in here. Keep the egg in the fire, 'cause their mothers breathe on 'em, see, an' when it hatches, feed it on a bucket o' brandy mixed with chicken blood every half hour."

Rubeus Hagrid

HARRY POTTER AND THE SORCERER'S STONE,
Chapter 14, "Norbert the Norwegian Ridgeback"

APRIL 25

"But there aren't wild dragons in *Britain*?" said Harry.

"Of course there are," said Ron. "Common Welsh Green and Hebridean Blacks. The Ministry of Magic has a job hushing them up, I can tell you. Our kind have to keep putting spells on Muggles who've spotted them, to make them forget."

HARRY POTTER AND THE SORCERER'S STONE,
Chapter 14, "Norbert the Norwegian Ridgeback"

APRIL 26

Dragons comprised entirely of green-and-gold sparks were soaring up and down the corridors, emitting loud fiery blasts and bangs as they went.

HARRY POTTER AND THE ORDER OF THE PHOENIX,
Chapter 28, "Snape's Worst Memory"

APRIL 27

"Well, here goes," said Harry, and he raised the little bottle and took a carefully measured gulp.

"What does it feel like?" whispered Hermione.

Harry did not answer for a moment. Then, slowly but surely, an exhilarating sense of infinite opportunity stole through him; he felt as though he could have done anything, anything at all . . .

HARRY POTTER AND THE HALF-BLOOD PRINCE,
Chapter 22, "After the Burial"

APRIL 28

PROFESSOR SLUGHORN'S BIRTHDAY

"Well," said Slughorn, not looking at Riddle, but fiddling with the ribbon on top of his box of crystalized pineapple, "well, it can't hurt to give you an overview, of course. Just so that you understand the term. A Horcrux is the word used for an object in which a person has concealed part of their soul."

HARRY POTTER AND THE HALF-BLOOD PRINCE,
Chapter 23, "Horcruxes"

APRIL 29

"Ah, Professor Snape," said Umbridge, smiling widely and standing up again. "Yes, I would like another bottle of Veritaserum, as quick as you can, please."

"You took my last bottle to interrogate Potter," he said, observing her coolly through his greasy curtains of black hair. "Surely you did not use it all? I told you that three drops would be sufficient."

HARRY POTTER AND THE ORDER OF THE PHOENIX,
Chapter 32, "Out of the Fire"

APRIL 30

"Professor, I'm really sorry to disturb you," said Harry as quietly as possible, while Ron stood on tiptoe, attempting to see past Slughorn into his room, "but my friend Ron's swallowed a love potion by mistake. You couldn't make him an antidote, could you? I'd take him to Madam Pomfrey, but we're not supposed to have anything from Weasleys' Wizard Wheezes and, you know . . . awkward questions . . ."

"I'd have thought you could have whipped him up a remedy, Harry, an expert potioneer like you?" asked Slughorn.

HARRY POTTER AND THE HALF-BLOOD PRINCE,
Chapter 18, "Birthday Surprises"

May

It was the first really fine day they'd had in months. The sky was a clear, forget-me-not blue, and there was a feeling in the air of summer coming.

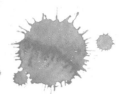

MAY 1

"We shall secure the school against He-Who-Must-Not-Be-Named while you search for this — this object."

"Is that possible?"

"I think so," said Professor McGonagall dryly, "we teachers are rather good at magic, you know."

HARRY POTTER AND THE DEATHLY HALLOWS,
Chapter 30, "The Sacking of Severus Snape"

MAY 2

BATTLE OF HOGWARTS

"Well, we do look to our prefects to take a lead at times such as these," said George in a good imitation of Percy's most pompous manner. "Now let's get upstairs and fight, or all the good Death Eaters'll be taken."

HARRY POTTER AND THE DEATHLY HALLOWS,
Chapter 30, "The Sacking of Severus Snape"

MAY 3

He moved down the steps and out into the darkness. It was nearly four in the morning, and the deathly stillness of the grounds felt as though they were holding their breath, waiting to see whether he could do what he must.

HARRY POTTER AND THE DEATHLY HALLOWS,
Chapter 34, "The Forest Again"

MAY 4

Grawp knelt between two trees he had not yet uprooted.
They looked up into his startlingly huge face, which resembled
a gray full moon swimming in the gloom of the clearing. It was
as though the features had been hewn onto a great stone ball.

HARRY POTTER AND THE ORDER OF THE PHOENIX,
Chapter 30, "Grawp"

MAY 5

"It's not easy ter catch a unicorn, they're powerful magic creatures."

Rubeus Hagrid

HARRY POTTER AND THE SORCERER'S STONE,
Chapter 15, "The Forbidden Forest"

MAY 6

So, with Fang scampering around them, sniffing tree roots and leaves, they entered the forest.

HARRY POTTER AND THE CHAMBER OF SECRETS,
Chapter 15, "Aragog"

MAY 7

There was suddenly a sound of more galloping from the other side of the clearing. Ronan and Bane came bursting through the trees, their flanks heaving and sweaty.

"Firenze!" Bane thundered. "What are you doing? You have a human on your back! Have you no shame? Are you a common mule?"

HARRY POTTER AND THE SORCERER'S STONE,
Chapter 15, "The Forbidden Forest"

MAY 8

"There he is, Mum, there he is, look!"

It was Ginny Weasley, Ron's younger sister, but she wasn't pointing at Ron.

"Harry Potter!" she squealed. "Look, Mum! I can see —"

HARRY POTTER AND THE SORCERER'S STONE,
Chapter 17, "The Man with Two Faces"

MAY 9

"Come on, Ginny's not bad," said George fairly, sitting down next to Fred. "Actually, I dunno how she got so good, seeing how we never let her play with us. . . ."

"She's been breaking into your broom shed in the garden since the age of six and taking each of your brooms out in turn when you weren't looking," said Hermione from behind her tottering pile of Ancient Rune books.

"Oh," said George, looking mildly impressed. "Well — that'd explain it."

HARRY POTTER AND THE ORDER OF THE PHOENIX,
Chapter 26, "Seen and Unforeseen"

MAY 10

Harry looked around; there was Ginny running toward him; she had a hard, blazing look in her face as she threw her arms around him. And without thinking, without planning it, without worrying about the fact that fifty people were watching, Harry kissed her.

HARRY POTTER AND THE HALF-BLOOD PRINCE,
Chapter 24, "Sectumsempra"

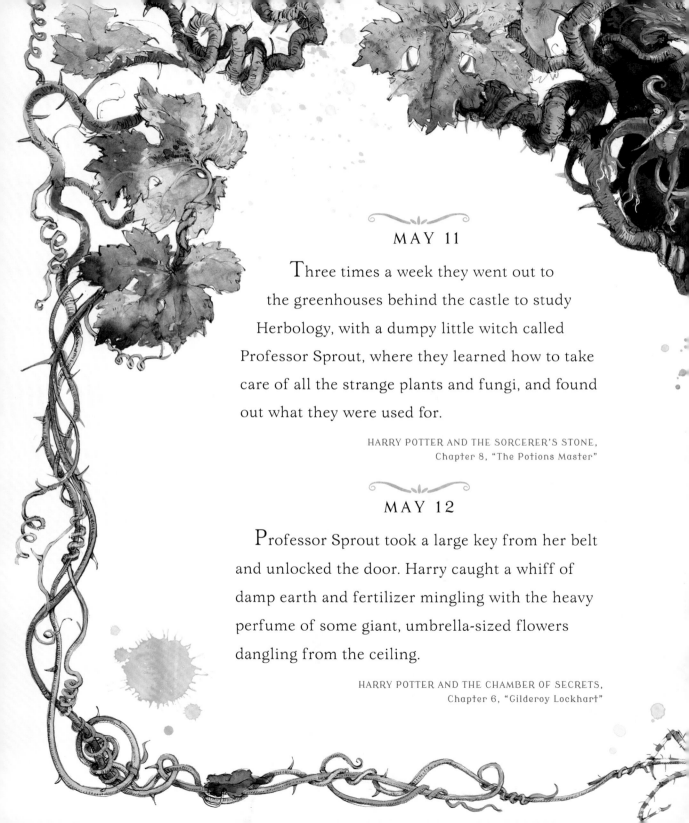

MAY 11

Three times a week they went out to
the greenhouses behind the castle to study
Herbology, with a dumpy little witch called
Professor Sprout, where they learned how to take
care of all the strange plants and fungi, and found
out what they were used for.

HARRY POTTER AND THE SORCERER'S STONE,
Chapter 8, "The Potions Master"

MAY 12

Professor Sprout took a large key from her belt
and unlocked the door. Harry caught a whiff of
damp earth and fertilizer mingling with the heavy
perfume of some giant, umbrella-sized flowers
dangling from the ceiling.

HARRY POTTER AND THE CHAMBER OF SECRETS,
Chapter 6, "Gilderoy Lockhart"

MAY 13

There was usually a large amount of earth on her clothes, and her fingernails would have made Aunt Petunia faint.

HARRY POTTER AND THE CHAMBER OF SECRETS,
Chapter 6, "Gilderoy Lockhart"

MAY 14

"Bubotubers," Professor Sprout told them briskly. "They need squeezing. You will collect the pus —"

"The *what*?" said Seamus Finnigan, sounding revolted.

"Pus, Finnigan, pus," said Professor Sprout, "and it's extremely valuable, so don't waste it."

HARRY POTTER AND THE GOBLET OF FIRE,
Chapter 13, "Mad-Eye Moody"

MAY 15

PROFESSOR SPROUT'S BIRTHDAY

And as she jogged out of sight, they could hear her muttering, "Tentacula. Devil's Snare. And Snargaluff pods . . . yes, I'd like to see the Death Eaters fighting those."

HARRY POTTER AND THE DEATHLY HALLOWS,
Chapter 30, "The Sacking of Severus Snape"

MAY 16

Broad strips of dazzling gold sunlight fell across the corridor from the high windows. The sky outside was so brightly blue it looked as though it had been enameled.

HARRY POTTER AND THE GOBLET OF FIRE,
Chapter 29, "The Dream"

MAY 17

Professor Trelawney bent down and lifted, from under her chair, a miniature model of the solar system, contained within a glass dome. It was a beautiful thing; each of the moons glimmered in place around the nine planets and the fiery sun, all of them hanging in thin air beneath the glass.

HARRY POTTER AND THE GOBLET OF FIRE,
Chapter 29, "The Dream"

MAY 18

"Well, now, this looks absolutely wonderful," said Slughorn an hour and a half later, clapping his hands together as he stared down into the sunshine-yellow contents of Harry's cauldron. "*Euphoria*, I take it? And what's that I smell? Mmmm . . . you've added just a sprig of peppermint, haven't you? Unorthodox, but what a stroke of inspiration, Harry . . ."

HARRY POTTER AND THE HALF-BLOOD PRINCE,
Chapter 22, "After the Burial"

MAY 19

The sun slipped lower in the sky, which was turning indigo; and still the dragon flew, cities and towns gliding out of sight beneath them, its enormous shadow sliding over the earth like a great dark cloud. Every part of Harry ached with the effort of holding on to the dragon's back.

HARRY POTTER AND THE DEATHLY HALLOWS,
Chapter 27, "The Final Hiding Place"

MAY 20

A shallow stone basin lay there, with odd carvings around the edge: runes and symbols that Harry did not recognize. The silvery light was coming from the basin's contents, which were like nothing Harry had ever seen before.

HARRY POTTER AND THE GOBLET OF FIRE,
Chapter 30, "The Pensieve"

MAY 21

He wanted to touch it, to find out what it felt like, but nearly four years' experience of the magical world told him that sticking his hand into a bowl full of some unknown substance was a very stupid thing to do.

HARRY POTTER AND THE GOBLET OF FIRE,
Chapter 30, "The Pensieve"

MAY 22

"Petunia says there isn't a Hogwarts. It *is* real, isn't it?"

"It's real for us," said Snape. "Not for her. But we'll get the letter, you and me."

"Really?" whispered Lily.

"Definitely," said Snape . . .

HARRY POTTER AND THE DEATHLY HALLOWS,
Chapter 33, "The Prince's Tale"

MAY 23

Dumbledore drew his wand out of the inside of his robes and placed the tip into his own silvery hair, near his temple. When he took the wand away, hair seemed to be clinging to it — but then Harry saw that it was in fact a glistening strand of the same strange silvery-white substance that filled the Pensieve.

HARRY POTTER AND THE GOBLET OF FIRE,
Chapter 30, "The Pensieve"

"*Open*," said Harry, in a low, faint hiss.

The serpents parted as the wall cracked open, the halves slid smoothly out of sight, and Harry, shaking from head to foot, walked inside.

HARRY POTTER AND THE CHAMBER OF SECRETS,
Chapter 16, "The Chamber of Secrets"

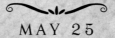

MAY 25

He was standing at the end of a very long, dimly lit chamber. Towering stone pillars entwined with more carved serpents rose to support a ceiling lost in darkness, casting long, black shadows through the odd, greenish gloom that filled the place.

HARRY POTTER AND THE CHAMBER OF SECRETS,
Chapter 17, "The Heir of Slytherin"

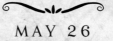

MAY 26

"I fashioned myself a new name, a name I knew wizards everywhere would one day fear to speak, when I had become the greatest sorcerer in the world!"

Tom Riddle

HARRY POTTER AND THE CHAMBER OF SECRETS,
Chapter 17, "The Heir of Slytherin"

MAY 27

He, Ron, and Hermione kept to themselves, working late into the night, trying to remember the ingredients in complicated potions, learn charms and spells by heart, memorize the dates of magical discoveries and goblin rebellions. . . .

HARRY POTTER AND THE SORCERER'S STONE,
Chapter 15, "The Forbidden Forest"

MAY 28

Chess was the only thing Hermione ever lost at, something Harry and Ron thought was very good for her.

HARRY POTTER AND THE SORCERER'S STONE,
Chapter 13, "Nicolas Flamel"

MAY 29

Professor McGonagall got to her feet too, and in her case this was a much more impressive move. She towered over Professor Umbridge.

"Potter," she said in ringing tones, "I will assist you to become an Auror if it is the last thing I do! If I have to coach you nightly I will make sure you achieve the required results!"

HARRY POTTER AND THE ORDER OF THE PHOENIX,
Chapter 29, "Career Advice"

MAY 30

Harry went to tip an armful of withered stalks onto the compost heap and found himself face-to-face with Ernie Macmillan. Ernie took a deep breath and said, very formally, "I just want to say, Harry, that I'm sorry I ever suspected you. I know you'd never attack Hermione Granger, and I apologize for all the stuff I said."

HARRY POTTER AND THE CHAMBER OF SECRETS,
Chapter 15, "Aragog"

MAY 31

Even the weather seemed to be celebrating; as June approached, the days became cloudless and sultry, and all anybody felt like doing was strolling onto the grounds and flopping down on the grass with several pints of iced pumpkin juice, perhaps playing a casual game of Gobstones or watching the giant squid propel itself dreamily across the surface of the lake.

HARRY POTTER AND THE PRISONER OF AZKABAN,
Chapter 16, "Professor Trelawney's Prediction"

June

The castle grounds were gleaming in the sunlight as though freshly painted; the cloudless sky smiled at itself in the smoothly sparkling lake, the satin-green lawns rippled occasionally in a gentle breeze.

JUNE 1

"Of course, it's not what you know," he was heard to tell Crabbe and Goyle loudly outside Potions a few days before the exams were to start, "it's who you know."

HARRY POTTER AND THE ORDER OF THE PHOENIX, Chapter 31, "O.W.L.s"

JUNE 2

"Longbottom, if brains were gold you'd be poorer than Weasley, and that's saying something." *Draco Malfoy*

HARRY POTTER AND THE SORCERER'S STONE, Chapter 13, "Nicolas Flamel"

JUNE 3

Even Fred and George Weasley had been spotted working; they were about to take their O.W.L.s (Ordinary Wizarding Levels). Percy was getting ready to take his N.E.W.T.s (Nastily Exhausting Wizarding Tests), the highest qualification Hogwarts offered.

HARRY POTTER AND THE PRISONER OF AZKABAN, Chapter 16, "Professor Trelawney's Prediction"

JUNE 4

Parvati was practicing incantations under her breath while the salt cellar in front of her twitched, Hermione was rereading *Achievement in Charming* so fast that her eyes appeared blurred, and Neville kept dropping his knife and fork and knocking over the marmalade.

HARRY POTTER AND THE ORDER OF THE PHOENIX,
Chapter 31, "O.W.L.s"

JUNE 5
DRACO MALFOY'S BIRTHDAY

"You'll soon find out some wizarding families are much better than others, Potter. You don't want to go making friends with the wrong sort. I can help you there."

Draco Malfoy

HARRY POTTER AND THE SORCERER'S STONE,
Chapter 6, "The Journey From Platform
Nine and Three-Quarters"

JUNE 6

"Auto-Answer Quills are banned from the examination hall, as are Remembralls, Detachable Cribbing Cuffs, and Self-Correcting Ink."

Minerva McGonagall

HARRY POTTER AND THE ORDER OF THE PHOENIX,
Chapter 31, "O.W.L.s"

JUNE 7

They had practical exams as well. Professor Flitwick called them one by one into his class to see if they could make a pineapple tap-dance across a desk.

HARRY POTTER AND THE SORCERER'S STONE,
Chapter 16, "Through the Trapdoor"

JUNE 8

"Now ... who'd like ter come an' visit the las' skrewt with me? I was jokin' — jokin'!" he added hastily, seeing the looks on their faces.

HARRY POTTER AND THE GOBLET OF FIRE,
Chapter 37, "The Beginning"

JUNE 9

The castle seemed very quiet even for a Sunday. Everybody was clearly out in the sunny grounds, enjoying the end of their exams and the prospect of a last few days of term unhampered by studying or homework.

HARRY POTTER AND THE ORDER OF THE PHOENIX,
Chapter 38, "The Second War Begins"

JUNE 10

"I am — I'm wearing the badge like Bill used to — and I'm holding the House Cup and the Quidditch Cup — I'm Quidditch captain, too!" *Ron Weasley*

HARRY POTTER AND THE SORCERER'S STONE,
Chapter 12, "The Mirror of Erised"

JUNE 11

The song was growing louder, but it was issuing not from a crowd of green-and-silver-clad Slytherins, but from a mass of red and gold moving slowly toward the castle, which was bearing a solitary figure upon its many shoulders....

"Weasley is our King,

Weasley is our King,

He didn't let the Quaffle in,

Weasley is our King . . ."

HARRY POTTER AND THE ORDER OF THE PHOENIX,
Chapter 30, "Grawp"

JUNE 12

Then Wood was speeding toward him, half-blinded by tears; he seized Harry around the neck and sobbed unrestrainedly into his shoulder. Harry felt two large thumps as Fred and George hit them; then Angelina's, Alicia's, and Katie's voices, *"We've won the Cup! We've won the Cup!"*

HARRY POTTER AND THE PRISONER OF AZKABAN,
Chapter 15, "The Quidditch Final"

JUNE 13

"Fawkes is a phoenix, Harry. Phoenixes burst into flame when it is time for them to die and are reborn from the ashes."

Albus Dumbledore

HARRY POTTER AND THE CHAMBER OF SECRETS,
Chapter 12, "The Polyjuice Potion"

JUNE 14

A crimson bird the size of a swan had appeared, piping its weird music to the vaulted ceiling. It had a glittering golden tail as long as a peacock's and gleaming golden talons, which were gripping a ragged bundle.

HARRY POTTER AND THE
CHAMBER OF SECRETS,
Chapter 17, "The Heir of Slytherin"

JUNE 15

The phoenix let out one soft, quavering note. It shivered in the air, and Harry felt as though a drop of hot liquid had slipped down his throat into his stomach, warming him, and strengthening him.

HARRY POTTER AND THE GOBLET OF FIRE,
Chapter 36, "The Parting of the Ways"

JUNE 16

"Harry's wand and Voldemort's wand share cores. Each of them contains a feather from the tail of the same phoenix. *This* phoenix, in fact," he added, and he pointed at the scarlet-and-gold bird, perching peacefully on Harry's knee.

HARRY POTTER AND THE GOBLET OF FIRE,
Chapter 36, "The Parting of the Ways"

JUNE 17

"What a year it has been! Hopefully your heads are all a little fuller than they were . . . you have the whole summer ahead to get them nice and empty before next year starts. . . ."

Albus Dumbledore

HARRY POTTER AND THE SORCERER'S STONE,
Chapter 17, "The Man with Two Faces"

JUNE 18

"There are all kinds of courage," said Dumbledore, smiling. "It takes a great deal of bravery to stand up to our enemies, but just as much to stand up to our friends. I therefore award ten points to Mr. Neville Longbottom."

HARRY POTTER AND THE SORCERER'S STONE,
Chapter 17, "The Man with Two Faces"

JUNE 19

Gryffindor house, meanwhile, largely thanks to their spectacular performance in the Quidditch Cup, had won the House Championship for the third year running. This meant that the end-of-term feast took place amid decorations of scarlet and gold, and that the Gryffindor table was the noisiest of the lot, as everybody celebrated.

HARRY POTTER AND THE PRISONER OF AZKABAN,
Chapter 22, "Owl Post Again"

JUNE 20

"Lord Voldemort's gift for spreading discord and enmity is very great. We can fight it only by showing an equally strong bond of friendship and trust. Differences of habit and language are nothing at all if our aims are identical and our hearts are open."

Albus Dumbledore

HARRY POTTER AND THE GOBLET OF FIRE,
Chapter 37, "The Beginning"

JUNE 21

"It is our choices, Harry, that show what we truly are, far more than our abilities."

Albus Dumbledore

HARRY POTTER AND THE CHAMBER OF SECRETS,
Chapter 18, "Dobby's Reward"

JUNE 22

"Call him Voldemort, Harry. Always use the proper name for things. Fear of a name increases fear of the thing itself."

Albus Dumbledore

HARRY POTTER AND THE SORCERER'S STONE,
Chapter 17, "The Man with Two Faces"

JUNE 23

"There will be obstacles," said Bagman happily, bouncing on the balls of his feet. "Hagrid is providing a number of creatures . . . then there will be spells that must be broken . . . all that sort of thing, you know."

HARRY POTTER AND THE GOBLET OF FIRE,
Chapter 28, "The Madness of Mr. Crouch"

JUNE 24
TRIWIZARD TOURNAMENT
THE THIRD TASK
DEATH OF CEDRIC DIGGORY

The Triwizard Cup was gleaming on a plinth a hundred yards away. Suddenly a dark figure hurtled out onto the path in front of him.

Cedric was going to get there first. Cedric was sprinting as fast as he could toward the cup, and Harry knew he would never catch up . . .

HARRY POTTER AND THE GOBLET OF FIRE,
Chapter 31, "The Third Task"

JUNE 25

"Both of us," Harry said.

"What?"

"We'll take it at the same time. It's still a Hogwarts victory. We'll tie for it."

Cedric stared at Harry. He unfolded his arms.

"You — you sure?"

HARRY POTTER AND THE GOBLET OF FIRE,
Chapter 31, "The Third Task"

JUNE 26

"There is much that I would like to say to you all tonight," said Dumbledore, "but I must first acknowledge the loss of a very fine person, who should be sitting here" — he gestured toward the Hufflepuffs — "enjoying our feast with us. I would like you all, please, to stand, and raise your glasses, to Cedric Diggory."

HARRY POTTER AND THE GOBLET OF FIRE,
Chapter 37, "The Beginning"

JUNE 27

When they reached the top of the Astronomy Tower at eleven
o'clock they found a perfect night for stargazing, cloudless and still.
The grounds were bathed in silvery moonlight,
and there was a slight chill in the air.

HARRY POTTER AND THE ORDER OF THE PHOENIX,
Chapter 31, "O.W.L.s"

JUNE 28

"Harry, you've got to come and
stay with us. I'll fix it up with Mum
and Dad, then I'll call you. I know
how to use a fellytone now — "

"A *telephone*, Ron," said
Hermione. "Honestly,
you should take Muggle
Studies next year...."

HARRY POTTER AND THE PRISONER OF AZKABAN,
Chapter 22, "Owl Post Again"

JUNE 29

And suddenly, their wardrobes were empty, their trunks were packed, Neville's toad was found lurking in a corner of the toilets; notes were handed out to all students, warning them not to use magic over the holidays ("I always hope they'll forget to give us these," said Fred Weasley sadly) . . .

HARRY POTTER AND THE SORCERER'S STONE,
Chapter 17, "The Man with Two Faces"

JUNE 30
BATTLE AT THE
ASTRONOMY TOWER
DEATH OF ALBUS DUMBLEDORE

"I will only *truly* have left this school when none here are loyal to me. You will also find that help will always be given at Hogwarts to those who ask for it."

Albus Dumbledore

HARRY POTTER AND THE CHAMBER OF SECRETS,
Chapter 14, "Cornelius Fudge"

July

The hottest day of the summer so far was drawing to a close and a drowsy silence lay over the large, square houses of Privet Drive.

JULY 1

He rolled onto his back and tried to remember the dream he had been having. It had been a good one. There had been a flying motorcycle in it. He had a funny feeling he'd had the same dream before.

HARRY POTTER AND THE SORCERER'S STONE,
Chapter 2, "The Vanishing Glass"

JULY 2

He'd lived with the Dursleys almost ten years, ten miserable years, as long as he could remember, ever since he'd been a baby and his parents had died in that car crash. He couldn't remember being in the car when his parents had died. Sometimes, when he strained his memory during long hours in his cupboard, he came up with a strange vision: a blinding flash of green light and a burning pain on his forehead.

HARRY POTTER AND THE SORCERER'S STONE,
Chapter 2, "The Vanishing Glass"

JULY 3

He missed Hogwarts so much it was
like having a constant stomachache.

HARRY POTTER AND THE CHAMBER OF SECRETS,
Chapter 1, "The Worst Birthday"

JULY 4

While Dudley lolled around watching and eating ice cream, Harry cleaned the windows, washed the car, mowed the lawn, trimmed the flower beds, pruned and watered the roses, and repainted the garden bench.

HARRY POTTER AND THE CHAMBER OF SECRETS,
Chapter 1, "The Worst Birthday"

JULY 5

"Duddy's got to make himself smart for his auntie," said Aunt Petunia, smoothing Dudley's thick blond hair. "Mummy's bought him a lovely new bow tie."

HARRY POTTER AND THE PRISONER OF AZKABAN,
Chapter 2, "Aunt Marge's Big Mistake"

JULY 6

"I'm not having one in the house, Petunia! Didn't we swear when we took him in we'd stamp out that dangerous nonsense?"

Vernon Dursley

HARRY POTTER AND THE SORCERER'S STONE, Chapter 3, "The Letters From No One"

JULY 7

"Godfather?" spluttered Uncle Vernon. "You haven't got a godfather!"

"Yes, I have," said Harry brightly. "He was my mum and dad's best friend. He's a convicted murderer, but he's broken out of wizard prison and he's on the run. He likes to keep in touch with me, though . . . keep up with my news . . . check I'm happy. . . ."

HARRY POTTER AND THE PRISONER OF AZKABAN, Chapter 22, "Owl Post Again"

JULY 8

Harry Potter was a highly unusual boy in many ways. For one thing, he hated the summer holidays more than any other time of year. For another, he really wanted to do his homework but was forced to do it in secret, in the dead of night.

HARRY POTTER AND THE PRISONER OF AZKABAN,
Chapter 1, "Owl Post"

JULY 9

Harry just had time to register its handsome green cover, emblazoned with the golden title *The Monster Book of Monsters*, before it flipped onto its edge and scuttled sideways along the bed like some weird crab.

HARRY POTTER AND THE PRISONER OF AZKABAN,
Chapter 1, "Owl Post"

JULY 10

"Vernon Dursley speaking."

Harry, who happened to be in the room at the time, froze as he heard Ron's voice answer.

"HELLO? HELLO? CAN YOU HEAR ME? I — WANT — TO — TALK — TO — HARRY — POTTER!"

HARRY POTTER AND THE PRISONER OF AZKABAN,
Chapter 1, "Owl Post"

JULY 11

His heart gave a huge bound as he ripped back the paper and saw a sleek black leather case, with silver words stamped across it, reading *Broomstick Servicing Kit.*

"Wow, Hermione!" Harry whispered, unzipping the case to look inside.

HARRY POTTER AND THE PRISONER OF AZKABAN,
Chapter 1, "Owl Post"

JULY 12

Hedwig hooted happily at Harry from her perch on top of a large wardrobe, then took off through the window; Harry knew she had been waiting to see him before going hunting.

HARRY POTTER AND THE HALF-BLOOD PRINCE,
Chapter 5, "An Excess of Phlegm"

JULY 13

We have received intelligence that a Hover Charm was used at your place of residence this evening at twelve minutes past nine.

Mafalda Hopkirk

HARRY POTTER AND THE CHAMBER OF SECRETS,
Chapter 2, "Dobby's Warning"

JULY 14

"EXPECTO PATRONUM!"

An enormous silver stag erupted from the tip of Harry's wand; its antlers caught the dementor in the place where the heart should have been; it was thrown backward, weightless as darkness, and as the stag charged, the dementor swooped away, batlike and defeated.

HARRY POTTER AND THE ORDER OF THE PHOENIX,
Chapter 1, "Dudley Demented"

JULY 15

"Keep your wand out," she told Harry, as they entered Wisteria Walk. "Never mind the Statute of Secrecy now, there's going to be hell to pay anyway, we might as well be hanged for a dragon as an egg."

Arabella Figg

HARRY POTTER AND THE ORDER OF THE PHOENIX,
Chapter 2, "A Peck of Owls"

JULY 16

"And now, Harry, let us step out into the night and pursue that flighty temptress, adventure."

Albus Dumbledore

HARRY POTTER AND THE HALF-BLOOD PRINCE,
Chapter 3, "Will and Won't"

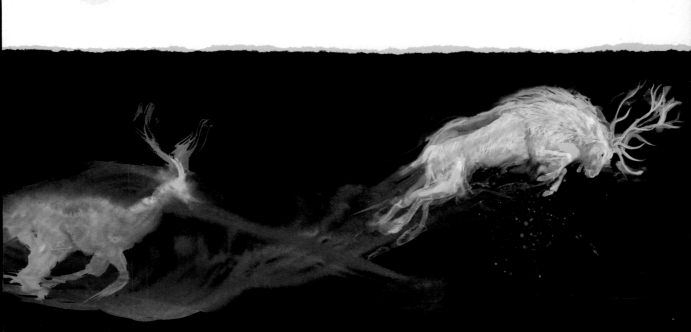

JULY 17

Life at the Burrow was as different as possible from life on Privet Drive. The Dursleys liked everything neat and ordered; the Weasleys' house burst with the strange and unexpected.

HARRY POTTER AND THE CHAMBER OF SECRETS,
Chapter 4, "At Flourish and Blotts"

JULY 18

Harry, Ron, Fred, and George were planning to go up the hill to a small paddock the Weasleys owned. It was surrounded by trees that blocked it from view of the village below, meaning that they could practice Quidditch there, as long as they didn't fly too high. They couldn't use real Quidditch balls, which would have been hard to explain if they had escaped and flown away over the village; instead they threw apples for one another to catch.

HARRY POTTER AND THE CHAMBER OF SECRETS,
Chapter 4, "At Flourish and Blotts"

JULY 19

The ghoul in the attic howled and dropped pipes whenever he felt things were getting too quiet, and small explosions from Fred and George's bedroom were considered perfectly normal.

HARRY POTTER AND THE CHAMBER OF SECRETS,
Chapter 4, "At Flourish and Blotts"

JULY 20

Behind Harry, the entrance to the marquee revealed rows and rows of fragile golden chairs set either side of a long purple carpet. The supporting poles were entwined with white and gold flowers. Fred and George had fastened an enormous bunch of golden balloons over the exact point where Bill and Fleur would shortly become husband and wife.

HARRY POTTER AND THE DEATHLY HALLOWS,
Chapter 8, "The Wedding"

JULY 21

Harry was feeling extremely well fed and at peace with the world as he watched several gnomes sprinting through the rosebushes, laughing madly and closely pursued by Crookshanks.

HARRY POTTER AND THE GOBLET OF FIRE,
Chapter 5, "Weasleys' Wizard Wheezes"

JULY 22

Aunt Petunia's masterpiece of a pudding, the mountain of cream and sugared violets, was floating up near the ceiling. On top of a cupboard in the corner crouched Dobby.

"No," croaked Harry. "Please . . . they'll kill me. . . ."

HARRY POTTER AND THE CHAMBER OF SECRETS,
Chapter 2, "Dobby's Warning"

JULY 23

"Mr. Weasley, it's Harry . . . the fireplace has been blocked up. You won't be able to get through there."

"Damn!" said Mr. Weasley's voice. "What on earth did they want to block up the fireplace for?"

HARRY POTTER AND THE GOBLET OF FIRE,
Chapter 4, "Back to the Burrow"

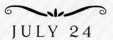

JULY 24

"*Jiggery pokery!*" said Harry in a fierce voice. "Hocus pocus — squiggly wiggly —"

"MUUUUUUM!" howled Dudley, tripping over his feet as he dashed back toward the house. "MUUUUM! He's doing you know what!"

HARRY POTTER AND THE CHAMBER OF SECRETS,
Chapter 1, "The Worst Birthday"

JULY 25

Hagrid seized his umbrella and whirled it over his head. "NEVER —" he thundered, "— INSULT — ALBUS — DUMBLEDORE — IN — FRONT — OF — ME!"

HARRY POTTER AND THE SORCERER'S STONE,
Chapter 4, "The Keeper of the Keys"

JULY 26

Uncle Vernon was pointing at what looked like a large rock way out at sea. Perched on top of the rock was the most miserable little shack you could imagine.

HARRY POTTER AND THE SORCERER'S STONE,
Chapter 3, "The Letters From No One"

JULY 27

Turning the envelope over, his hand trembling, Harry saw a purple wax seal bearing a coat of arms; a lion, an eagle, a badger, and a snake surrounding a large letter *H*.

HARRY POTTER AND THE SORCERER'S STONE,
Chapter 3, "The Letters From No One"

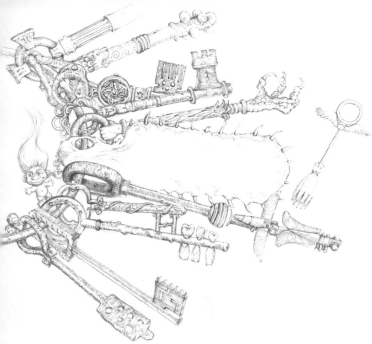

JULY 28

"Las' time I saw you, you was only a baby," said the giant. "Yeh look a lot like yer dad, but yeh've got yer mum's eyes."

Rubeus Hagrid

HARRY POTTER AND THE SORCERER'S STONE,
Chapter 4, "The Keeper of the Keys"

JULY 29

From an inside pocket of his black overcoat he pulled a slightly squashed box. Harry opened it with trembling fingers. Inside was a large, sticky chocolate cake with *Happy Birthday Harry* written on it in green icing.

HARRY POTTER AND THE SORCERER'S STONE,
Chapter 4, "The Keeper of the Keys"

JULY 30
NEVILLE LONGBOTTOM'S BIRTHDAY

"We're all going to keep fighting, Harry. You know that?"

Neville Longbottom

HARRY POTTER AND THE DEATHLY HALLOWS,
Chapter 34, "The Forest Again"

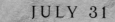
HARRY POTTER'S BIRTHDAY

"Harry — yer a wizard."

There was silence inside the hut. Only the
sea and the whistling wind could be heard.

"I'm a *what*?" gasped Harry.

HARRY POTTER AND THE SORCERER'S STONE,
Chapter 4, "The Keeper of the Keys"

August

Mr. Weasley conjured up candles to light the darkening garden before they had their homemade strawberry ice cream, and by the time they had finished, moths were fluttering low over the table and the warm air was perfumed with the smells of grass and honeysuckle.

AUGUST 1

Four or five chimneys were perched on top of the red roof. A lopsided sign stuck in the ground near the entrance read *The Burrow*. Around the front door lay a jumble of rubber boots and a very rusty cauldron. Several fat brown chickens were pecking their way around the yard.

HARRY POTTER AND THE CHAMBER OF SECRETS,
Chapter 3, "The Burrow"

AUGUST 2

Harry stepped over a pack of Self-Shuffling playing cards on the floor and looked out of the tiny window. In the field far below he could see a gang of gnomes sneaking one by one back through the Weasleys' hedge.

HARRY POTTER AND THE CHAMBER OF SECRETS,
Chapter 3, "The Burrow"

AUGUST 3

Books were stacked three deep on the mantelpiece, books with titles like *Charm Your Own Cheese*, *Enchantment in Baking*, and *One Minute Feasts — It's Magic!* And unless Harry's ears were deceiving him, the old radio next to the sink had just announced that coming up was "Witching Hour, with the popular singing sorceress, Celestina Warbeck."

HARRY POTTER AND THE CHAMBER OF SECRETS,
Chapter 3, "The Burrow"

AUGUST 4

By seven o'clock, the two tables were groaning under dishes and dishes of Mrs. Weasley's excellent cooking, and the nine Weasleys, Harry, and Hermione were settling themselves down to eat beneath a clear, deep-blue sky.

HARRY POTTER AND THE GOBLET OF FIRE,
Chapter 5, "Weasleys' Wizard Wheezes"

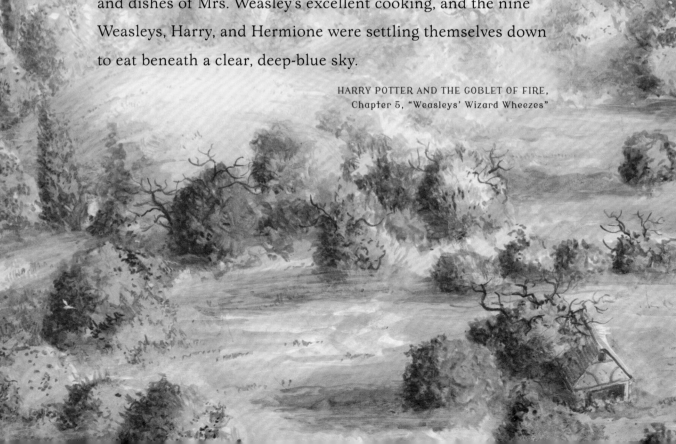

AUGUST 5

"Can we buy all this in London?" Harry wondered aloud.

"If yeh know where to go," said Hagrid.

HARRY POTTER AND THE SORCERER'S STONE,
Chapter 5, "Diagon Alley"

AUGUST 6

"Three up . . . two across . . ." he muttered. "Right, stand back, Harry."

He tapped the wall three times with the point of his umbrella.

The brick he had touched quivered — it wriggled — in the middle, a small hole appeared — it grew wider and wider — a second later they were facing an archway large enough even for Hagrid, an archway onto a cobbled street that twisted and turned out of sight.

"Welcome," said Hagrid, "to Diagon Alley."

HARRY POTTER AND THE SORCERER'S STONE,
Chapter 5, "Diagon Alley"

AUGUST 7

Harry, Ron, and Hermione strolled off along the winding, cobbled street. The bag of gold, silver, and bronze jangling cheerfully in Harry's pocket was clamoring to be spent, so he bought three large strawberry-and-peanut-butter ice creams, which they slurped happily as they wandered up the alley, examining the fascinating shop windows.

HARRY POTTER AND THE CHAMBER OF SECRETS,
Chapter 4, "At Flourish and Blotts"

AUGUST 8

A loud ripping noise rent the air; two of the *Monster Books* had seized a third and were pulling it apart.

"Stop it! Stop it!" cried the manager, poking the walking stick through the bars and knocking the books apart. "I'm never stocking them again, never! It's been bedlam! I thought we'd seen the worst when we bought two hundred copies of *The Invisible Book of Invisibility* — cost a fortune, and we never found them...."

HARRY POTTER AND THE PRISONER OF AZKABAN,
Chapter 4, "The Leaky Cauldron"

AUGUST 9

"Curious indeed how these things happen. The wand chooses the wizard, remember.... I think we must expect great things from you, Mr. Potter...."
Garrick Ollivander

HARRY POTTER AND THE SORCERER'S STONE,
Chapter 5, "Diagon Alley"

AUGUST 10

A low, soft hooting came from a dark shop with a sign saying *Eeylops Owl Emporium — Tawny, Screech, Barn, Brown, and Snowy.* Several boys of about Harry's age had their noses pressed against a window with broomsticks in it. "Look," Harry heard one of them say, "the new Nimbus Two Thousand — fastest ever —" There were shops selling robes, shops selling telescopes and strange silver instruments Harry had never seen before, windows stacked with barrels of bat spleens and eels' eyes, tottering piles of spell books, quills, and rolls of parchment, potion bottles, globes of the moon. . . .

HARRY POTTER AND THE SORCERER'S STONE,
Chapter 5, "Diagon Alley"

AUGUST 11

"Yeah, the D.A.'s good," said Ginny. "Only let's make it stand for Dumbledore's Army because that's the Ministry's worst fear, isn't it?"

HARRY POTTER AND THE ORDER OF THE PHOENIX,
Chapter 18, "Dumbledore's Army"

AUGUST 12

"I don't believe it! I don't believe it! Oh, Ron, how wonderful! A prefect! That's everyone in the family!"

"What are Fred and I, next-door neighbors?" said George indignantly, as his mother pushed him aside and flung her arms around her youngest son.

HARRY POTTER AND THE ORDER OF THE PHOENIX,
Chapter 9, "The Woes of Mrs. Weasley"

AUGUST 13

Harry saw Mrs. Weasley glance at the clock in the washing basket as they left the kitchen. All the hands were once again at "mortal peril."

HARRY POTTER AND THE HALF-BLOOD PRINCE,
Chapter 5, "An Excess of Phlegm"

AUGUST 14

Mrs. Weasley jabbed her wand at the cutlery drawer, which shot open. Harry and Ron both jumped out of the way as several knives soared out of it, flew across the kitchen, and began chopping the potatoes, which had just been tipped back into the sink by the dustpan.

HARRY POTTER AND THE GOBLET OF FIRE,
Chapter 5, "Weasleys' Wizard Wheezes"

AUGUST 15

"Welcome to the Knight Bus, emergency transport for the stranded witch or wizard. Just stick out your wand hand, step on board, and we can take you anywhere you want to go. My name is Stan Shunpike, and I will be your conductor this eve —"

The conductor stopped abruptly. He had just caught sight of Harry, who was still sitting on the ground.

HARRY POTTER AND THE PRISONER OF AZKABAN,
Chapter 3, "The Knight Bus"

AUGUST 16

"Listen, how much would it be to get to London?"

"Eleven Sickles," said Stan, "but for firteen you get 'ot chocolate, and for fifteen you get an 'ot-water bottle an' a toofbrush in the color of your choice."

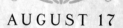

HARRY POTTER AND THE PRISONER OF AZKABAN,
Chapter 3, "The Knight Bus"

AUGUST 17

One by one, wizards and witches in dressing gowns and slippers descended from the upper floors to leave the bus. They all looked very pleased to go.

HARRY POTTER AND THE PRISONER OF AZKABAN,
Chapter 3, "The Knight Bus"

AUGUST 18

"I knew it!" Stan shouted gleefully. "Ern! Ern! Guess 'oo Neville is, Ern! 'E's 'Arry Potter! I can see 'is scar!"

HARRY POTTER AND THE PRISONER OF AZKABAN,
Chapter 3, "The Knight Bus"

AUGUST 19

"And this is Nymphadora — "

"*Don't* call me Nymphadora, Remus," said
the young witch with a shudder. "It's Tonks."

"— Nymphadora Tonks, who prefers to be
known by her surname only," finished Lupin.

"So would you if your fool of a mother had
called you 'Nymphadora,' muttered Tonks.

HARRY POTTER AND THE ORDER OF THE PHOENIX,
Chapter 3, "The Advance Guard"

AUGUST 20

"Kingsley Shacklebolt's been a real asset too. He's in charge of the hunt for
Sirius, so he's been feeding the Ministry information that Sirius is in Tibet."

Arthur Weasley

HARRY POTTER AND THE ORDER OF THE PHOENIX,
Chapter 5, "The Order of the Phoenix"

AUGUST 21

"Oh, my dear boy, we're not going to punish you for a little thing like
that!" cried Fudge, waving his crumpet impatiently. "It was an accident!
We don't send people to Azkaban just for blowing up their aunts!"

HARRY POTTER AND THE PRISONER OF AZKABAN,
Chapter 3, "The Knight Bus"

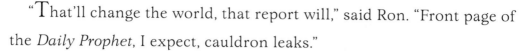
AUGUST 22
PERCY WEASLEY'S BIRTHDAY

"That'll change the world, that report will," said Ron. "Front page of the *Daily Prophet*, I expect, cauldron leaks."

Percy went slightly pink.

"You might sneer, Ron," he said heatedly, "but unless some sort of international law is imposed we might well find the market flooded with flimsy, shallow-bottomed products that seriously endanger —"

HARRY POTTER AND THE GOBLET OF FIRE,
Chapter 5, "Weasleys' Wizard Wheezes"

AUGUST 23

When Cornelius Fudge, the Minister for Magic himself, arrived, Percy bowed so low that his glasses fell off and shattered. Highly embarrassed, he repaired them with his wand and thereafter remained in his seat, throwing jealous looks at Harry, whom Cornelius Fudge had greeted like an old friend.

HARRY POTTER AND THE GOBLET OF FIRE,
Chapter 8, "The Quidditch World Cup"

AUGUST 24

Now, with the sun newly risen and the mist lifting, they could see the city of tents that stretched in every direction.

HARRY POTTER AND THE GOBLET OF FIRE,
Chapter 7, "Bagman and Crouch"

AUGUST 25

Though Ron purchased a dancing shamrock hat and a large green rosette, he also bought a small figure of Viktor Krum, the Bulgarian Seeker. The miniature Krum walked backward and forward over Ron's hand, scowling up at the green rosette above him.

HARRY POTTER AND THE GOBLET OF FIRE,
Chapter 7, "Bagman and Crouch"

AUGUST 26

"Ladies and gentlemen . . . welcome! Welcome to the final of the four hundred and twenty-second Quidditch World Cup!"

The spectators screamed and clapped. Thousands of flags waved, adding their discordant national anthems to the racket. The huge blackboard opposite them was wiped clear of its last message (*Bertie Bott's Every Flavor Beans — A Risk with Every Mouthful!*) and now showed BULGARIA: 0, IRELAND: 0.

HARRY POTTER AND THE GOBLET OF FIRE,
Chapter 8, "The Quidditch World Cup"

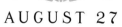

AUGUST 27

"He's got it — Krum's got it — it's all over!" shouted Harry.

Krum, his red robes shining with blood from his nose, was rising gently into the air, his fist held high, a glint of gold in his hand.

HARRY POTTER AND THE GOBLET OF FIRE,
Chapter 8, "The Quidditch World Cup"

AUGUST 28

The moment he had got wind of the fact that he was expected to survive the summer on carrot sticks, Harry had sent Hedwig to his friends with pleas for help, and they had risen to the occasion magnificently.

HARRY POTTER AND THE GOBLET OF FIRE,
Chapter 3, "The Invitation"

AUGUST 29

It would be best for Harry to send us your answer
as quickly as possible in the normal way, because the
Muggle postman has never delivered to our house,
and I am not sure he even knows where it is.

Hoping to see Harry soon,

Yours sincerely,

Molly Weasley

P.S. I do hope we've put enough stamps on.

HARRY POTTER AND THE GOBLET OF FIRE,
Chapter 3, "The Invitation"

AUGUST 30

"No, Harry, *you* listen," said Hermione. "We're coming with you. That was decided months ago — years, really."

"But — "

"Shut up," Ron advised him.

HARRY POTTER AND THE DEATHLY HALLOWS,
Chapter 6, "The Ghoul in Pajamas"

AUGUST 31

On their last evening, Mrs. Weasley conjured up a sumptuous dinner that included all of Harry's favorite things, ending with a mouth-watering treacle pudding. Fred and George rounded off the evening with a display of Filibuster fireworks; they filled the kitchen with red and blue stars that bounced from ceiling to wall for at least half an hour.

HARRY POTTER AND THE CHAMBER OF SECRETS,
Chapter 5, "The Whomping Willow"

September

Smoke from the engine drifted over the heads
of the chattering crowd, while cats of every color
wound here and there between their legs. Owls hooted
to one another in a disgruntled sort of way over
the babble and the scraping of heavy trunks.

SEPTEMBER 1

"All you have to do is walk straight at the barrier between platforms nine and ten. Don't stop and don't be scared you'll crash into it, that's very important. Best do it at a bit of a run if you're nervous. Go on, go now before Ron." *Molly Weasley*

HARRY POTTER AND THE SORCERER'S STONE,
Chapter 6, "The Journey From Platform Nine and Three-Quarters"

SEPTEMBER 2

"Gran, I've lost my toad again."

"Oh, *Neville*," he heard the old woman sigh.

HARRY POTTER AND THE SORCERER'S STONE,
Chapter 6, "The Journey From Platform Nine and Three-Quarters"

SEPTEMBER 3

"Go on, have a pasty," said Harry, who had never had anything to share before or, indeed, anyone to share it with. It was a nice feeling, sitting there with Ron, eating their way through all Harry's pasties, cakes, and candies . . . (the sandwiches lay forgotten).

HARRY POTTER AND THE SORCERER'S STONE,
Chapter 6, "The Journey From Platform Nine and Three-Quarters"

SEPTEMBER 4

When darkness fell and lamps came on inside the carriages, Luna rolled up *The Quibbler*, put it carefully away in her bag, and took to staring at everyone in the compartment instead.

HARRY POTTER AND THE ORDER OF THE PHOENIX,
Chapter 10, "Luna Lovegood"

SEPTEMBER 5

And the fleet of little boats moved off all at once, gliding across the lake, which was as smooth as glass. Everyone was silent, staring up at the great castle overhead.

HARRY POTTER AND THE SORCERER'S STONE,
Chapter 6, "The Journey From Platform Nine and Three-Quarters"

SEPTEMBER 6

"Welcome to Hogwarts," said Professor McGonagall. "The start-of-term banquet will begin shortly, but before you take your seats in the Great Hall, you will be sorted into your houses. The Sorting is a very important ceremony because, while you are here, your house will be something like your family within Hogwarts."

HARRY POTTER AND THE SORCERER'S STONE,
Chapter 7, "The Sorting Hat"

SEPTEMBER 7

"Before we begin our banquet, I would like to say a few words. And here they are: Nitwit! Blubber! Oddment! Tweak!" *Albus Dumbledore*

HARRY POTTER AND THE SORCERER'S STONE,
Chapter 7, "The Sorting Hat"

SEPTEMBER 8

"*Now slip me snug about your ears,*
I've never yet been wrong,
I'll have a look inside your mind
And tell where you belong!"
The Sorting Hat

HARRY POTTER AND THE GOBLET OF FIRE,
Chapter 12, "The Triwizard Tournament"

SEPTEMBER 9

At the very end of the corridor hung a portrait of a very fat woman in a pink silk dress.

"Password?" she said.

"*Caput Draconis*," said Percy, and the portrait swung forward to reveal a round hole in the wall. They all scrambled through it — Neville needed a leg up — and found themselves in the Gryffindor common room, a cozy, round room full of squashy armchairs.

HARRY POTTER AND THE SORCERER'S STONE,
Chapter 7, "The Sorting Hat"

SEPTEMBER 10

Harry climbed the spiral stairs with no thought in his head except how glad he was to be back. They reached their familiar, circular dormitory with its five four-poster beds, and Harry, looking around, felt he was home at last.

HARRY POTTER AND THE PRISONER OF AZKABAN,
Chapter 5, "The Dementor"

SEPTEMBER 11

Harry had caught Ron prodding Dean's poster of West Ham soccer team, trying to make the players move.

HARRY POTTER AND THE SORCERER'S STONE,
Chapter 9, "The Midnight Duel"

SEPTEMBER 12

Harry looked across the now empty common room and saw, illuminated by the moonlight, a snowy owl perched on the windowsill.

"Hedwig!" he shouted, and he launched himself out of his chair and across the room to pull open the window.

HARRY POTTER AND THE GOBLET OF FIRE,
Chapter 14, "The Unforgivable Curses"

SEPTEMBER 13

There were a hundred and forty-two staircases at Hogwarts: wide, sweeping ones; narrow, rickety ones; some that led somewhere different on a Friday; some with a vanishing step halfway up that you had to remember to jump.

HARRY POTTER AND THE SORCERER'S STONE,
Chapter 8, "The Potions Master"

SEPTEMBER 14

"Wandering around at midnight, Ickle Firsties? Tut, tut, tut. Naughty, naughty, you'll get caughty."

"Not if you don't give us away, Peeves, please."

"Should tell Filch, I should," said Peeves in a saintly voice, but his eyes glittered wickedly. "It's for your own good, you know."

HARRY POTTER AND THE SORCERER'S STONE,
Chapter 9, "The Midnight Duel"

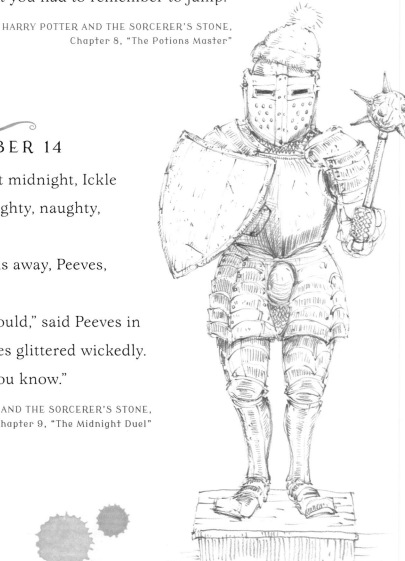

SEPTEMBER 15

Then there were doors that wouldn't open unless you asked politely, or tickled them in exactly the right place, and doors that weren't really doors at all, but solid walls just pretending. It was also very hard to remember where anything was, because it all seemed to move around a lot. The people in the portraits kept going to visit each other and Harry was sure the coats of armor could walk.

HARRY POTTER AND THE SORCERER'S STONE,
Chapter 8, "The Potions Master"

SEPTEMBER 16

"But Hogwarts *is* hidden," said Hermione, in surprise. "Everyone knows that . . . well, everyone who's read *Hogwarts: A History*, anyway."

"Just you, then," said Ron. "So go on — how d'you hide a place like Hogwarts?"

"It's bewitched," said Hermione. "If a Muggle looks at it, all they see is a moldering old ruin with a sign over the entrance saying *DANGER, DO NOT ENTER, UNSAFE*."

HARRY POTTER AND THE GOBLET OF FIRE,
Chapter 11, "Aboard the Hogwarts Express"

SEPTEMBER 17

"Nobody in my family's magic at all, it was ever such a surprise when I got my letter, but I was ever so pleased, of course, I mean, it's the very best school of witchcraft there is, I've heard — I've learned all our course books by heart, of course, I just hope it will be enough — I'm Hermione Granger, by the way, who are you?"

She said all this very fast.

HARRY POTTER AND THE SORCERER'S STONE,
Chapter 6, "The Journey From Platform Nine and Three-Quarters"

SEPTEMBER 18

But from that moment on, Hermione Granger became their friend. There are some things you can't share without ending up liking each other, and knocking out a twelve-foot mountain troll is one of them.

HARRY POTTER AND THE SORCERER'S STONE,
Chapter 10, "Halloween"

SEPTEMBER 19

HERMIONE GRANGER'S BIRTHDAY

"I hope you're pleased with yourselves. We could all have been killed — or worse, expelled. Now, if you don't mind, I'm going to bed."

Hermione Granger

HARRY POTTER AND THE SORCERER'S STONE,
Chapter 9, "The Midnight Duel"

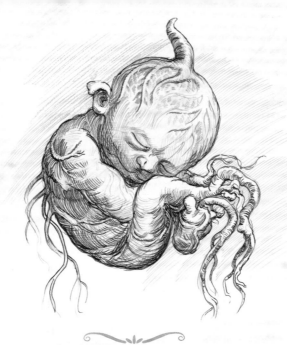

SEPTEMBER 20

There was a lot more to magic, as Harry quickly found out, than waving your wand and saying a few funny words.

HARRY POTTER AND THE SORCERER'S STONE,
Chapter 8, "The Potions Master"

SEPTEMBER 21

Professor Sprout dusted off her hands, gave them all the thumbs-up, and removed her own earmuffs.

"As our Mandrakes are only seedlings, their cries won't kill yet," she said calmly as though she'd just done nothing more exciting than water a begonia.

HARRY POTTER AND THE CHAMBER OF SECRETS,
Chapter 6, "Gilderoy Lockhart"

SEPTEMBER 22

"Four to a tray — there is a large supply of pots here — compost in the sacks over there — and be careful of the Venomous Tentacula, it's teething."

She gave a sharp slap to a spiky, dark red plant as she spoke, making it draw in the long feelers that had been inching sneakily over her shoulder.

HARRY POTTER AND THE CHAMBER OF SECRETS,
Chapter 6, "Gilderoy Lockhart"

SEPTEMBER 23

It was lucky that Harry had tea with Hagrid to look forward to, because the Potions lesson turned out to be the worst thing that had happened to him so far.

HARRY POTTER AND THE SORCERER'S STONE,
Chapter 8, "The Potions Master"

SEPTEMBER 24

"Would you care for a lemon drop?"

"A *what*?"

"A lemon drop. They're a kind of
Muggle sweet I'm rather fond of."

HARRY POTTER AND THE SORCERER'S STONE,
Chapter 1, "The Boy Who Lived"

SEPTEMBER 25

"Scars can come in handy. I have one myself above my left knee that is
a perfect map of the London Underground." *Albus Dumbledore*

HARRY POTTER AND THE SORCERER'S STONE,
Chapter 1, "The Boy Who Lived"

SEPTEMBER 26

"Ah, music," he said, wiping his eyes. "A magic beyond
all we do here!" *Albus Dumbledore*

HARRY POTTER AND THE SORCERER'S STONE,
Chapter 7, "The Sorting Hat"

SEPTEMBER 27

"Of course it is happening inside your head, Harry, but why on
earth should that mean that it is not real?" *Albus Dumbledore*

HARRY POTTER AND THE DEATHLY HALLOWS,
Chapter 35, "King's Cross"

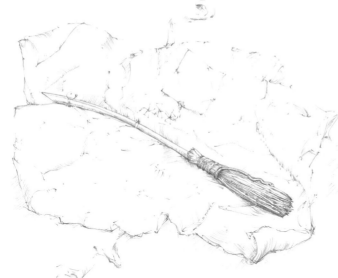

He mounted the broom
and kicked hard against the
ground and up, up he soared;
air rushed through his hair, and
his robes whipped out behind
him — and in a rush of fierce joy
he realized he'd found something
he could do without being taught — this
was easy, this was *wonderful.*

HARRY POTTER AND THE SORCERER'S STONE,
Chapter 9, "The Midnight Duel"

SEPTEMBER 29

Malfoy certainly did talk about flying a lot. He
complained loudly about first years never getting
on the house Quidditch teams and told long,
boastful stories that always seemed to end with him
narrowly escaping Muggles in helicopters.

HARRY POTTER AND THE SORCERER'S STONE,
Chapter 9, "The Midnight Duel"

SEPTEMBER 30

Professor McGonagall peered sternly over her glasses at Harry.

"I want to hear you're training hard, Potter, or I may change my mind about punishing you."

Then she suddenly smiled.

"Your father would have been proud," she said. "He was an excellent Quidditch player himself."

HARRY POTTER AND THE SORCERER'S STONE,
Chapter 9, "The Midnight Duel"

October

*Raindrops the size of bullets thundered
on the castle windows for days on end:
the lake rose, the flower beds turned into
muddy streams, and Hagrid's pumpkins
swelled to the size of garden sheds.*

OCTOBER 1

Hagrid's big, hairy face appeared in
the crack as he pulled the door open.
"Hang on," he said. "*Back*, Fang."
He let them in, struggling to keep
a hold on the collar of an enormous
black boarhound.

HARRY POTTER AND THE SORCERER'S STONE,
Chapter 8, "The Potions Master"

OCTOBER 2

A light rain had started to fall by midafternoon;
it was very cozy sitting by the fire, listening to
the gentle patter of the drops on the window,
watching Hagrid darning his socks and arguing with
Hermione about house-elves — for he flatly refused
to join S.P.E.W. when she showed him her badges.

HARRY POTTER AND THE GOBLET OF FIRE,
Chapter 16, "The Goblet of Fire"

In the small vegetable patch behind Hagrid's house were a dozen of the largest pumpkins Harry had ever seen. Each was the size of a large boulder.

"Gettin' on well, aren't they?" said Hagrid happily. "Fer the Halloween feast . . . should be big enough by then."

"What've you been feeding them?" said Harry.

Hagrid looked over his shoulder to check that they were alone.

"Well, I've bin givin' them — you know — a bit o' help —"

Harry noticed Hagrid's flowery pink umbrella leaning against the back wall of the cabin.

HARRY POTTER AND THE CHAMBER OF SECRETS,
Chapter 7, "Mudbloods and Murmurs"

OCTOBER 4

"How did you know it was me?" she asked.

"My dear Professor, I've never seen a cat sit so stiffly."

"You'd be stiff if you'd been sitting on a brick wall all day," said Professor McGonagall.

HARRY POTTER AND THE SORCERER'S STONE,
Chapter 1, "The Boy Who Lived"

OCTOBER 5

"Transfiguration is some of the most complex and dangerous magic you will learn at Hogwarts," she said. "Anyone messing around in my class will leave and not come back. You have been warned."

Then she changed her desk into a pig and back again. They were all very impressed and couldn't wait to get started, but soon realized they weren't going to be changing the furniture into animals for a long time. After taking a lot of complicated notes, they were each given a match and started trying to turn it into a needle. By the end of the lesson, only Hermione Granger had made any difference to her match; Professor McGonagall showed the class how it had gone all silver and pointy and gave Hermione a rare smile.

HARRY POTTER AND THE SORCERER'S STONE,
Chapter 8, "The Potions Master"

OCTOBER 6

The third years emerged from Transfiguration at lunchtime on Monday, limp and ashen-faced, comparing results and bemoaning the difficulty of the tasks they had been set, which had included turning a teapot into a tortoise.

HARRY POTTER AND THE PRISONER OF AZKABAN,
Chapter 16, "Professor Trelawney's Prediction"

OCTOBER 7

"All in favor of the D.A.?" said Hermione bossily, kneeling up on her cushion to count. "That's a majority — motion passed!"

She pinned the piece of paper with all of their names on it on the wall and wrote DUMBLEDORE'S ARMY across the top in large letters.

HARRY POTTER AND THE ORDER OF THE PHOENIX,
Chapter 18, "Dumbledore's Army"

OCTOBER 8

"We think the reason Umbridge doesn't want us trained in Defense Against the Dark Arts," said Hermione, "is that she's got some . . . some mad idea that Dumbledore could use the students in the school as a kind of private army. She thinks he'd mobilize us against the Ministry."

HARRY POTTER AND THE ORDER OF THE PHOENIX,
Chapter 16, "In the Hog's Head"

OCTOBER 9

The walls were lined with wooden bookcases, and instead of chairs there were large silk cushions on the floor. A set of shelves at the far end of the room carried a range of instruments such as Sneakoscopes, Secrecy Sensors, and a large, cracked Foe-Glass that Harry was sure had hung, the previous year, in the fake Moody's office.

HARRY POTTER AND THE ORDER OF THE PHOENIX,
Chapter 18, "Dumbledore's Army"

OCTOBER 10

"*Expelliarmus!*" said Neville, and Harry, caught unawares, felt his wand fly out of his hand.

"I DID IT!" said Neville gleefully. "I've never done it before — I DID IT!"

HARRY POTTER AND THE ORDER OF THE PHOENIX,
Chapter 18, "Dumbledore's Army"

OCTOBER 11

Rain was still lashing the windows, which were now inky black, but inside all looked bright and cheerful. The firelight glowed over the countless squashy armchairs where people sat reading, talking, doing homework or, in the case of Fred and George Weasley, trying to find out what would happen if you fed a Filibuster firework to a salamander.

HARRY POTTER AND THE CHAMBER OF SECRETS,
Chapter 8, "The Deathday Party"

OCTOBER 12

Crookshanks wandered over to them, leapt lightly into an empty chair, and stared inscrutably at Harry, rather as Hermione might look if she knew they weren't doing their homework properly.

HARRY POTTER AND THE GOBLET OF FIRE,
Chapter 14, "The Unforgivable Curses"

OCTOBER 13

"Does he have to eat that in front of us?" said Ron, scowling.

"Clever Crookshanks, did you catch that all by yourself?" said Hermione.

Crookshanks slowly chewed up the spider, his yellow eyes fixed insolently on Ron.

HARRY POTTER AND THE PRISONER OF AZKABAN,
Chapter 8, "Flight of the Fat Lady"

OCTOBER 14

"CATCH THAT CAT!" Ron yelled as Crookshanks freed himself from the remnants of the bag, sprang over the table, and chased after the terrified Scabbers.

HARRY POTTER AND THE PRISONER OF AZKABAN,
Chapter 8, "Flight of the Fat Lady"

OCTOBER 15

The Snitch he had caught earlier was now zooming around and around the common room; people were watching its progress as though hypnotized and Crookshanks was leaping from chair to chair, trying to catch it.

HARRY POTTER AND THE ORDER OF THE PHOENIX,
Chapter 19, "The Lion and the Serpent"

187

OCTOBER 16

They watched the birds soaring overhead, glittering — *glittering*? "They're not birds!" Harry said suddenly. "They're *keys*! Winged keys — look carefully."

HARRY POTTER AND THE SORCERER'S STONE,
Chapter 16, "Through the Trapdoor"

OCTOBER 17

PROFESSOR FLITWICK'S BIRTHDAY

"Now, don't forget that nice wrist movement we've been practicing!" squeaked Professor Flitwick, perched on top of his pile of books as usual. "Swish and flick, remember, swish and flick. And saying the magic words properly is very important, too — never forget Wizard Baruffio, who said 's' instead of 'f' and found himself on the floor with a buffalo on his chest."

HARRY POTTER AND THE SORCERER'S STONE,
Chapter 10, "Halloween"

OCTOBER 18

Hermione rolled up the sleeves of her gown, flicked her wand, and said, "*Wingardium Leviosa!*"

Their feather rose off the desk and hovered about four feet above their heads.

HARRY POTTER AND THE SORCERER'S STONE,
Chapter 10, "Halloween"

OCTOBER 19

The teachers were, of course, forbidden from mentioning the interview by Educational Decree Number Twenty-six, but they found ways to express their feelings about it all the same. Professor Sprout awarded Gryffindor twenty points when Harry passed her a watering can; a beaming Professor Flitwick pressed a box of squeaking sugar mice on him at the end of Charms, said *"Shh!"* and hurried away . . .

HARRY POTTER AND THE ORDER OF THE PHOENIX,
Chapter 26, "Seen and Unforeseen"

OCTOBER 20

Harry saw, with immense satisfaction, a disheveled and soot-blackened Umbridge tottering sweaty-faced from Professor Flitwick's classroom.

"Thank you so much, Professor!" said Professor Flitwick in his squeaky little voice. "I could have got rid of the sparklers myself, of course, but I wasn't sure whether I had the *authority. . . ."*

Beaming, he closed his classroom door in her snarling face.

HARRY POTTER AND THE ORDER OF THE PHOENIX,
Chapter 28, "Snape's Worst Memory"

OCTOBER 21

Madam Pomfrey, the nurse, was kept busy by a sudden spate of colds among the staff and students. Her Pepperup Potion worked instantly, though it left the drinker smoking at the ears for several hours afterward.

HARRY POTTER AND THE CHAMBER OF SECRETS,
Chapter 8, "The Deathday Party"

OCTOBER 22

"First Hogsmeade weekend," said Ron, pointing at a notice that had appeared on the battered old bulletin board. "End of October. Halloween."

HARRY POTTER AND THE PRISONER OF AZKABAN,
Chapter 8, "Flight of the Fat Lady"

OCTOBER 23

He and Ron spent much of Sunday catching up with all their homework again, and although this could hardly be called fun, the last burst of autumn sunshine persisted, so rather than sitting hunched over tables in the common room, they took their work outside and lounged in the shade of a large beech tree on the edge of the lake.

HARRY POTTER AND THE ORDER OF THE PHOENIX,
Chapter 17, "Educational Decree Number Twenty-Four"

OCTOBER 24

"Well, this Halloween will be my five hundredth deathday," said Nearly Headless Nick, drawing himself up and looking dignified.

"Oh," said Harry, not sure whether he should look sorry or happy about this. "Right."

HARRY POTTER AND THE CHAMBER OF SECRETS,
Chapter 8, "The Deathday Party"

OCTOBER 25

"I'm holding a party down in one of the roomier dungeons. Friends will be coming from all over the country. It would be such an *honor* if you would attend."

Nearly Headless Nick

HARRY POTTER AND THE CHAMBER OF SECRETS,
Chapter 8, "The Deathday Party"

OCTOBER 26

The dungeon was full of hundreds of pearly-white, translucent people, mostly drifting around a crowded dance floor, waltzing to the dreadful, quavering sound of thirty musical saws, played by an orchestra on a raised, black-draped platform.

HARRY POTTER AND THE CHAMBER OF SECRETS,
Chapter 8, "The Deathday Party"

OCTOBER 27

Large, rotten fish were laid on handsome silver platters; cakes, burned charcoal black, were heaped on salvers; there was a great maggoty haggis, a slab of cheese covered in furry green mold and, in pride of place, an enormous gray cake in the shape of a tombstone, with tar-like icing forming the words,

SIR NICHOLAS DE MIMSY-PORPINGTON, DIED 31ST OCTOBER, 1492

HARRY POTTER AND THE CHAMBER OF SECRETS,
Chapter 8, "The Deathday Party"

OCTOBER 28

On Halloween morning they woke to the delicious smell of baking pumpkin wafting through the corridors.

HARRY POTTER AND THE SORCERER'S STONE,
Chapter 10, "Halloween"

OCTOBER 29

The rest of the school was happily anticipating their Halloween feast; the Great Hall had been decorated with the usual live bats, Hagrid's vast pumpkins had been carved into lanterns large enough for three men to sit in, and there were rumors that Dumbledore had booked a troupe of dancing skeletons for the entertainment.

HARRY POTTER AND THE CHAMBER OF SECRETS,
Chapter 8, "The Deathday Party"

OCTOBER 30

MOLLY WEASLEY'S BIRTHDAY

Mrs. Weasley set the potion down on the bedside cabinet, bent down, and put her arms around Harry. He had no memory of ever being hugged like this, as though by a mother.

HARRY POTTER AND THE GOBLET OF FIRE,
Chapter 36, "The Parting of the Ways"

OCTOBER 31

HALLOWEEN
NEARLY HEADLESS NICK DEATHDAY

The feast finished with an entertainment provided by the Hogwarts ghosts. They popped out of the walls and tables to do a bit of formation gliding; Nearly Headless Nick, the Gryffindor ghost, had a great success with a reenactment of his own botched beheading.

HARRY POTTER AND THE PRISONER OF AZKABAN,
Chapter 8, "Flight of the Fat Lady"

November

As they entered November, the weather turned very cold. The mountains around the school became icy gray and the lake like chilled steel. Every morning the ground was covered in frost.

NOVEMBER 1

For one brief moment, the great black dog reared onto its hind legs and placed its front paws on Harry's shoulders, but Mrs. Weasley shoved Harry away toward the train door hissing, "For heaven's sake act more like a dog, Sirius!"

HARRY POTTER AND THE ORDER OF THE PHOENIX,
Chapter 10, "Luna Lovegood"

NOVEMBER 2

Sirius, who was right beside Harry, let out his usual barklike laugh.

"No one would have made me a prefect, I spent too much time in detention with James. Lupin was the good boy, he got the badge."

HARRY POTTER AND THE ORDER OF THE PHOENIX,
Chapter 9, "The Woes of Mrs. Weasley"

NOVEMBER 3

SIRIUS BLACK'S BIRTHDAY

"If you want to know what a man's like, take a good look at how he treats his inferiors, not his equals."

Sirius Black

HARRY POTTER AND THE GOBLET OF FIRE,
Chapter 27, "Padfoot Returns"

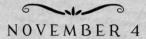

NOVEMBER 4

"Believe me, Harry. I never betrayed James and Lily. I would have died before I betrayed them."

Sirius Black

HARRY POTTER AND THE PRISONER OF AZKABAN,
Chapter 19, "The Servant of Lord Voldemort"

NOVEMBER 5

The noise of the storm was even louder in the common room. Harry knew better than to think the match would be canceled; Quidditch matches weren't called off for trifles like thunderstorms.

HARRY POTTER AND THE PRISONER OF AZKABAN,
Chapter 9, "Grim Defeat"

NOVEMBER 6

On Madam Hooch's whistle, Harry kicked hard into the air and heard the telltale whoosh of the Bludger behind him.

HARRY POTTER AND THE CHAMBER OF SECRETS,
Chapter 10, "The Rogue Bludger"

NOVEMBER 7

Many people were staring at her and a few openly laughing and pointing; she had managed to procure a hat shaped like a life-size lion's head, which was perched precariously on her head.

"I'm supporting Gryffindor," said Luna, pointing unnecessarily at her hat. "Look what it does. . . ."

She reached up and tapped the hat with her wand. It opened its mouth wide and gave an extremely realistic roar that made everyone in the vicinity jump.

HARRY POTTER AND THE ORDER OF THE PHOENIX,
Chapter 19, "The Lion and the Serpent"

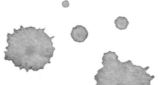

NOVEMBER 8

"And so," finished Slughorn, "I want each of you to come and take one of these phials from my desk. You are to create an antidote for the poison within it before the end of the lesson. Good luck, and don't forget your protective gloves!"

HARRY POTTER AND THE HALF-BLOOD PRINCE,
Chapter 18, "Birthday Surprises"

NOVEMBER 9

They were wincing as they dabbed essence of dittany onto their many injuries.

HARRY POTTER AND THE DEATHLY HALLOWS,
Chapter 27, "The Final Hiding Place"

NOVEMBER 10

They had brought cakes, sweets, and bottles of pumpkin juice; they gathered around Harry's bed and were just getting started on what promised to be a good party when Madam Pomfrey came storming over, shouting, "This boy needs rest, he's got thirty-three bones to regrow! Out! OUT!"

HARRY POTTER AND THE CHAMBER OF SECRETS,
Chapter 10, "The Rogue Bludger"

NOVEMBER 11

"Well, he should have some chocolate, at the very least," said Madam Pomfrey, who was now trying to peer into Harry's eyes.

"I've already had some," said Harry. "Professor Lupin gave me some. He gave it to all of us."

"Did he, now?" said Madam Pomfrey approvingly. "So we've finally got a Defense Against the Dark Arts teacher who knows his remedies."

HARRY POTTER AND THE PRISONER OF AZKABAN,
Chapter 5, "The Dementor"

NOVEMBER 12

Professor Snape was forcing them to research antidotes. They took this seriously, as he had hinted that he might be poisoning one of them before Christmas to see if their antidote worked.

HARRY POTTER AND THE GOBLET OF FIRE,
Chapter 15, "Beauxbatons and Durmstrang"

NOVEMBER 13

"Why don't we go and have a butterbeer in
the Three Broomsticks, it's a bit cold, isn't it?"
Hermione Granger

HARRY POTTER AND THE GOBLET OF FIRE,
Chapter 19, "The Hungarian Horntail"

NOVEMBER 14

They left Zonko's with their money bags considerably lighter than
they had been on entering, but their pockets bulging with Dungbombs,
Hiccup Sweets, Frog Spawn Soap, and a Nose-Biting Teacup apiece.

HARRY POTTER AND THE PRISONER OF AZKABAN,
Chapter 14, "Snape's Grudge"

NOVEMBER 15

The owls sat hooting softly down at him, at least three hundred of them; from Great Grays right down to tiny little Scops owls ("Local Deliveries Only"), which were so small they could have sat in the palm of Harry's hand.

HARRY POTTER AND THE PRISONER OF AZKABAN,
Chapter 14, "Snape's Grudge"

"You see, we have never been able
to keep a Defense Against the Dark Arts
teacher for longer than a year since I
refused the post to Lord Voldemort."

Albus Dumbledore

HARRY POTTER AND THE HALF-BLOOD PRINCE,
Chapter 20, "Lord Voldemort's Request"

NOVEMBER 17

"I did think of Voldemort first," said Harry honestly.
"But then I — I remembered those dementors."

"I see," said Lupin thoughtfully. "Well, well . . . I'm
impressed." He smiled slightly at the look of surprise
on Harry's face. "That suggests that what you fear
most of all is — fear. Very wise, Harry."

HARRY POTTER AND THE PRISONER OF AZKABAN,
Chapter 8, "Flight of the Fat Lady"

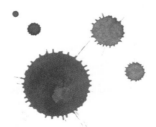

NOVEMBER 18

"Now, if there's no countercurse, why am I showing you? *Because you've got to know.* You've got to appreciate what the worst is. You don't want to find yourself in a situation where you're facing it. CONSTANT VIGILANCE!"

Mad-Eye Moody

HARRY POTTER AND THE GOBLET OF FIRE,
Chapter 14, "The Unforgivable Curses"

NOVEMBER 19

"All I could find was this, in the introduction to *Magick Moste Evile* — listen — 'of the Horcrux, wickedest of magical inventions, we shall not speak nor give direction'...." *Hermione Granger*

HARRY POTTER AND THE HALF-BLOOD PRINCE,
Chapter 18, "Birthday Surprises"

NOVEMBER 20

The skies and the ceiling of the Great Hall turned a pale, pearly gray, the mountains around Hogwarts became snowcapped, and the temperature in the castle dropped so far that many students wore their thick protective dragon skin gloves in the corridors between lessons.

HARRY POTTER AND THE ORDER OF THE PHOENIX,
Chapter 19, "The Lion and the Serpent"

NOVEMBER 21

It was very hard to move through crowds in the Invisibility Cloak, in case you accidentally trod on someone, which tended to lead to awkward questions.

HARRY POTTER AND THE GOBLET OF FIRE,
Chapter 19, "The Hungarian Horntail"

NOVEMBER 22

"What would your head have been doing in Hogsmeade, Potter?" said Snape softly. "Your head is not allowed in Hogsmeade. No part of your body has permission to be in Hogsmeade."

HARRY POTTER AND THE PRISONER OF AZKABAN,
Chapter 14, "Snape's Grudge"

NOVEMBER 23

"Coming through, coming through!" Percy called from behind the crowd. "The new password's 'Fortuna Major'!"

"Oh no," said Neville Longbottom sadly. He always had trouble remembering the passwords.

HARRY POTTER AND THE PRISONER OF AZKABAN,
Chapter 5, "The Dementor"

NOVEMBER 24

It was time to do what he had to do . . . to focus his mind, entirely and absolutely, upon the thing that was his only chance. . . .

He raised his wand.

"Accio Firebolt!" he shouted.

HARRY POTTER AND THE GOBLET OF FIRE,
Chapter 20, "The First Task"

NOVEMBER 25

"Keep back there, Hagrid!" yelled a wizard near the fence, straining on the chain he was holding. "They can shoot fire at a range of twenty feet, you know! I've seen this Horntail do forty!"

"Is'n' it beautiful?" said Hagrid softly.

HARRY POTTER AND THE GOBLET OF FIRE,
Chapter 19, "The Hungarian Horntail"

NOVEMBER 26

Cedric put his hand into the bag, and out came the blueish-gray Swedish Short-Snout, the number one tied around its neck. Knowing what was left, Harry put his hand into the silk bag and pulled out the Hungarian Horntail, and the number four.

HARRY POTTER AND THE GOBLET OF FIRE,
Chapter 20, "The First Task"

NOVEMBER 27

And there was the Horntail, at the other end of the enclosure, crouched low over her clutch of eggs, her wings half-furled, her evil, yellow eyes upon him, a monstrous, scaly, black lizard, thrashing her spiked tail, leaving yard-long gouge marks in the hard ground.

HARRY POTTER AND THE GOBLET OF FIRE,
Chapter 20, "The First Task"

SWEDISH SHORT-SNOUT

"They'll all forget this in a few weeks. Fred and George have lost loads of points in all the time they've been here, and people still like them."

"They've never lost a hundred and fifty points in one go, though, have they?" said Harry miserably.

"Well — no," Ron admitted.

HARRY POTTER AND THE SORCERER'S STONE,
Chapter 15, "The Forbidden Forest"

NOVEMBER 29

"It's just a pity they let the old punishments die out . . . hang you by your wrists from the ceiling for a few days, I've got the chains still in my office, keep 'em well oiled in case they're ever needed. . . ."

Argus Filch

HARRY POTTER AND THE SORCERER'S STONE,
Chapter 15, "The Forbidden Forest"

NOVEMBER 30

"I was never a prefect myself," said Tonks brightly from behind Harry as everybody moved toward the table to help themselves to food. Her hair was tomato red and waist-length today; she looked like Ginny's older sister. "My Head of House said I lacked certain necessary qualities."

"Like what?" said Ginny, who was choosing a baked potato.

"Like the ability to behave myself," said Tonks.

HARRY POTTER AND THE ORDER OF THE PHOENIX,
Chapter 9, "The Woes of Mrs. Weasley"

December

Snow was swirling against
the icy windows once more;
Christmas was approaching fast.

DECEMBER 1

One morning in mid-December, Hogwarts woke
to find itself covered in several feet of snow.

HARRY POTTER AND THE SORCERER'S STONE,
Chapter 12, "The Mirror of Erised"

DECEMBER 2

George closed the door quietly and then turned, beaming, to look at Harry.
"Early Christmas present for you, Harry," he said.

Fred pulled something from inside his cloak with a flourish and laid it
on one of the desks. It was a large, square, very worn piece of parchment
with nothing written on it. Harry, suspecting one of Fred and George's
jokes, stared at it.

HARRY POTTER AND THE PRISONER OF AZKABAN,
Chapter 10, "The Marauder's Map"

DECEMBER 3

Hogsmeade looked like a Christmas card; the little thatched cottages and shops were all covered in a layer of crisp snow; there were holly wreaths on the doors and strings of enchanted candles hanging in the trees.

HARRY POTTER AND THE PRISONER OF AZKABAN,
Chapter 10, "The Marauder's Map"

DECEMBER 4

"We can do all our Christmas shopping there!" said Hermione. "Mum and Dad would really love those Toothflossing Stringmints from Honeydukes!"

HARRY POTTER AND THE PRISONER OF AZKABAN,
Chapter 10, "The Marauder's Map"

DECEMBER 5

"I would trust Hagrid with my life," said Dumbledore.

HARRY POTTER AND THE SORCERER'S STONE,
Chapter 1, "The Boy Who Lived"

RUBEUS HAGRID'S BIRTHDAY

"I am what I am, an' I'm not ashamed. 'Never be ashamed,' my ol' dad used ter say, 'there's some who'll hold it against you, but they're not worth botherin' with.'"

Rubeus Hagrid

HARRY POTTER AND THE GOBLET OF FIRE,
Chapter 24, "Rita Skeeter's Scoop"

DECEMBER 7

The dormitory doors flew open, making them all jump: Hagrid came striding toward them, his hair rain-flecked, his bearskin coat flapping behind him, a crossbow in his hand, leaving a trail of muddy dolphin-sized footprints all over the floor.

HARRY POTTER AND THE HALF-BLOOD PRINCE,
Chapter 19, "Elf Tails"

DECEMBER 8

"I was at Hogwarts meself but I — er — got expelled, ter tell yeh the truth. In me third year. They snapped me wand in half an' everything."

Rubeus Hagrid

HARRY POTTER AND THE SORCERER'S STONE,
Chapter 4, "The Keeper of the Keys"

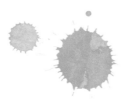

DECEMBER 9

"Now, Professor Dumbledore has granted me permission to start this little dueling club to train you all in case you ever need to defend yourselves as I myself have done on countless occasions — for full details, see my published works."

Gilderoy Lockhart

HARRY POTTER AND THE CHAMBER OF SECRETS,
Chapter 11, "The Dueling Club"

DECEMBER 10

The bell was due to ring at any moment, and Harry and Ron, who had been having a sword fight with a couple of Fred and George's fake wands at the back of the class, looked up, Ron holding a tin parrot, and Harry, a rubber haddock.

HARRY POTTER AND THE GOBLET OF FIRE,
Chapter 22, "The Unexpected Task"

DECEMBER 11

"Unusual combination — holly and phoenix feather, eleven inches, nice and supple."

Garrick Ollivander

HARRY POTTER AND THE SORCERER'S STONE,
Chapter 5, "Diagon Alley"

DECEMBER 12

He laid the broken wand upon the headmaster's desk, touched it with the very tip of the Elder Wand, and said, *"Reparo."*

As his wand resealed, red sparks flew out of its end. Harry knew that he had succeeded.

HARRY POTTER AND THE DEATHLY HALLOWS,
Chapter 36, "The Flaw in the Plan"

DECEMBER 13

"That wand's more trouble than it's worth," said Harry. "And quite honestly," he turned away from the painted portraits, thinking now only of the four-poster bed lying waiting for him in Gryffindor Tower, and wondering whether Kreacher might bring him a sandwich there, "I've had enough trouble for a lifetime."

HARRY POTTER AND THE DEATHLY HALLOWS,
Chapter 36, "The Flaw in the Plan"

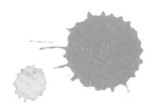

DECEMBER 14

Thick streamers of holly and mistletoe were strung along the corridors, mysterious lights shone from inside every suit of armor, and the Great Hall was filled with its usual twelve Christmas trees, glittering with golden stars.

HARRY POTTER AND THE PRISONER OF AZKABAN,
Chapter 11, "The Firebolt"

DECEMBER 15

"You try putting up tinsel when Peeves has got the other end and is trying to strangle you with it," said Ron.

HARRY POTTER AND THE ORDER OF THE PHOENIX,
Chapter 21, "The Eye of the Snake"

DECEMBER 16

"The Yule Ball is of course a chance for us all to — er — let our hair down," she said, in a disapproving voice.

Minerva McGonagall

HARRY POTTER AND THE GOBLET OF FIRE,
Chapter 22, "The Unexpected Task"

DECEMBER 17

"Mistletoe," said Cho quietly, pointing at the ceiling over his head.

"Yeah," said Harry. His mouth was very dry. "It's probably full of nargles, though."

HARRY POTTER AND THE ORDER OF THE PHOENIX,
Chapter 21, "The Eye of the Snake"

DECEMBER 18

"It's a shame you had to see him on a Burning Day," said Dumbledore, seating himself behind his desk. "He's really very handsome most of the time, wonderful red and gold plumage. Fascinating creatures, phoenixes. They can carry immensely heavy loads, their tears have healing powers, and they make highly *faithful* pets."

HARRY POTTER AND THE CHAMBER OF SECRETS,
Chapter 12, "The Polyjuice Potion"

DECEMBER 19

"I do feel so sorry," said Draco Malfoy, one Potions class, "for all those people who have to stay at Hogwarts for Christmas because they're not wanted at home."

HARRY POTTER AND THE SORCERER'S STONE,
Chapter 12, "The Mirror of Erised"

DECEMBER 20

They sat by the hour eating anything they could spear on a toasting fork — bread, English muffins, marshmallows — and plotting ways of getting Malfoy expelled, which were fun to talk about even if they wouldn't work.

HARRY POTTER AND THE SORCERER'S STONE,
Chapter 12, "The Mirror of Erised"

DECEMBER 21

Buckbeak the hippogriff was lying in the corner, chomping on something that was oozing blood all over the floor.

"I couldn' leave him tied up out there in the snow!" choked Hagrid. "All on his own! At Christmas!"

HARRY POTTER AND THE PRISONER OF AZKABAN,
Chapter 11, "The Firebolt"

DECEMBER 22

Ron also started teaching Harry wizard chess. This was exactly like Muggle chess except that the figures were alive, which made it a lot like directing troops in battle.

HARRY POTTER AND THE SORCERER'S STONE,
Chapter 12, "The Mirror of Erised"

DECEMBER 23

Mrs. Weasley had sent him a scarlet sweater with the Gryffindor lion knitted on the front; also a dozen home-baked mince pies, some Christmas cake, and a box of nut brittle.

HARRY POTTER AND THE PRISONER OF AZKABAN,
Chapter 11, "The Firebolt"

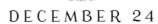

DECEMBER 24

"Crackers!" said Dumbledore enthusiastically, offering the end of a large silver noisemaker to Snape, who took it reluctantly and tugged. With a bang like a gunshot, the cracker flew apart to reveal a large, pointed witch's hat topped with a stuffed vulture.

HARRY POTTER AND THE PRISONER OF AZKABAN,
Chapter 11, "The Firebolt"

DECEMBER 25

CHRISTMAS DAY

Harry had never in all his life had such a Christmas dinner. A hundred fat, roast turkeys; mountains of roast and boiled potatoes; platters of chipolatas; tureens of buttered peas, silver boats of thick, rich gravy and cranberry sauce . . .

HARRY POTTER AND THE SORCERER'S STONE,
Chapter 12, "The Mirror of Erised"

DECEMBER 26

Something fluid and silvery gray went slithering to the floor, where it lay in gleaming folds. Ron gasped.

"I've heard of those," he said in a hushed voice, dropping the box of Every Flavor Beans he'd gotten from Hermione. "If that's what I think it is — they're really rare, and *really* valuable."

HARRY POTTER AND THE SORCERER'S STONE, Chapter 12, "The Mirror of Erised"

DECEMBER 27

Harry was so close to the mirror now that his nose was nearly touching that of his reflection.

"Mum?" he whispered. "Dad?"

HARRY POTTER AND THE SORCERER'S STONE, Chapter 12, "The Mirror of Erised"

DECEMBER 28

"The Mirror will be moved to a new home tomorrow, Harry, and I ask you not to go looking for it again. If you ever *do* run across it, you will now be prepared. It does not do to dwell on dreams and forget to live, remember that. Now, why don't you put that admirable Cloak back on and get off to bed?"

Albus Dumbledore

HARRY POTTER AND THE SORCERER'S STONE, Chapter 12, "The Mirror of Erised"

DECEMBER 29

He had awoken to find the
dormitory deserted, dressed, and gone
down the spiral staircase to a common room
that was completely empty except for Ron, who was eating
a Peppermint Toad and massaging his stomach, and
Hermione, who had spread her homework over three tables.

HARRY POTTER AND THE PRISONER OF AZKABAN,
Chapter 11, "The Firebolt"

DECEMBER 30

At that moment, Hedwig swooped into the room, carrying a very small package in her beak.

"Hello," said Harry happily as she landed on his bed. "Are you speaking to me again?"

She nibbled his ear in an affectionate sort of way, which was a far better present than the one that she had brought him, which turned out to be from the Dursleys. They had sent Harry a toothpick and a note telling him to find out whether he'd be able to stay at Hogwarts for the summer vacation, too.

HARRY POTTER AND THE CHAMBER OF SECRETS,
Chapter 12, "The Polyjuice Potion"

DECEMBER 31

TOM RIDDLE'S BIRTHDAY

"It is a curious thing, Harry, but perhaps those who are best suited to power are those who have never sought it. Those who, like you, have leadership thrust upon them, and take up the mantle because they must, and find to their own surprise that they wear it well."

Albus Dumbledore

HARRY POTTER AND THE DEATHLY HALLOWS,
Chapter 35, "King's Cross"

List of illustrations

In general I'm not particularly fussy about materials. I'm very fond of decorator's paint
for example — cheap and cheerful! — but, for simplicity's sake, let's call all the many
paints I use "watercolor." Many images have been tweaked digitally too.

Jim Kay

The Great Hall

The Kitchens

HARRY POTTER
Concept Work 2013
HOGWARTS

J.K. ROWLING is the author of the seven Harry Potter books, which have sold over 500 million copies, been translated into over 80 languages, and made into eight blockbuster films. She also wrote three short series companion volumes for charity, including *Fantastic Beasts and Where to Find Them*, which later became the inspiration for a new series of films. Harry's story as a grown-up was later continued in a stage play, *Harry Potter and the Cursed Child*, which J.K. Rowling wrote with playwright Jack Thorne and director John Tiffany.

In 2020, she returned to publishing for younger children with the fairy tale *The Ickabog*, which she initially published for free online for children in lockdown, later donating all her book royalties to her charitable trust, Volant, to help vulnerable groups affected by the Covid-19 pandemic.

J.K. Rowling has received many awards and honors for her writing, including for her detective series written under the name Robert Galbraith. She supports a wide number of humanitarian causes through Volant, and is the founder of the international children's care reform charity Lumos.

For as long as she can remember, J.K. Rowling wanted to be a writer, and is at her happiest in a room, making things up. She lives in Scotland with her family.

JIM KAY won the Kate Greenaway Medal in 2012 for his illustrations in *A Monster Calls* by Patrick Ness. He studied illustration at the University of Westminster, and worked in the Library & Archives of Tate Britain and then as an assistant curator of botanical illustrations at the Royal Botanic Gardens at Kew before returning to producing art full-time. After a one-man exhibition at Richmond Gallery he was approached by a publisher and his freelance career began. Alongside his illustration work, Jim has produced concept work for film and television, and contributed to the group exhibition *Memory Palace* at the V&A Museum in London. Jim lives and works in Sussex with his wife.